Darkest Communion

MICHELE E. GWYNN

AN M.E. GWYNN PUBLICATION

Contents

The Agony of Loneliness

1 356 A.D. Moldova

Perfume is never so sweet, so delicate as when it blends with the heat of her skin, the scent of her blood. Like the night sky, her memory intoxicates me, sitting upon my tongue like the finest wine, purifying my soul with her very essence. The craving to taste her red nectar overwhelms my sanity like waves from the deepest ocean, and the need to satisfy my craving sanctifies my spirit like darkest communion. However will I spend eternity without her by my side, without her light and her love? I am lost inside this hell without my sweet Mihaela…

Marku Andrei Anghelescu

Chapter 1

*B*ucharest, Romania, Present Day

Mark Anghelescu sat brooding over his computer. It was 2:00 a.m. and the worry line between his dark brows seemed more pronounced than usual. He was reading an article online about a group of students who had come to Romania to teach English at the University of Bucharest. The story itself was not interesting, but what kept Mark glued to the monitor was the picture posted of the students.

She stood in the center of the frame, surrounded by four others. Her face, radiant. Her eyes staring back at him seemed luminous, dark, and deep. Her smile promised laughter. He knew this face; knew it well although he hadn't gazed upon it for almost eight hundred years. Mark lifted a finger to trace a lock of the honey-colored hair that fell over her shoulder. The LCD screen distorted at the point of his touch.

It just couldn't be her, he thought. This vision from a long-forgotten past couldn't possibly be her. But the pain in his chest, the one that threatened to suffocate him with its intensity, told him otherwise. He felt...something; something both foreign and familiar, and he didn't like it. He hadn't felt anything for so long that the shock of feeling such pain...what was it? Grief! This feeling of grief was ripping him in two.

Memories bombarded him without mercy. Mihaela pressed against his flesh, locked onto him in passion. The sound of her pleasure being ripped from her as he mastered her body. The taste of her kiss as she licked his lips, nibbled his jaw, and whispered hotly in his ear, "More!"

It had sounded more like a moan than a command. But he accommodated her regardless, cradling her head in his hand and hiking her hips higher while burying himself deeper, pushing harder. Her lust had matched his own, fanning flames of passion so hot they consumed them both. And like two phoenixes, they arose from their own ashes in the morning and stoked the fire anew.

"Mihaela," whispered Mark. "My Mihaela."

He ran his hands through his wavy, dark hair before covering his face. There he sat, statue still, for nearly half an hour. His body shook subtly, as if sobbing, but no tears fell. He had none to shed.

Finally, Mark slid his hands down to his chin, resting his face in his palms and gazed once again at her image.

"I lost you once, but not this time. Fate, Mihaela, has brought you back to me." A slow smile spread across his ruggedly handsome face. An unholy light began to glow amber in his black eyes. He stood and stretched up to his full height of six foot five inches and flexed his broad shoulders. Then, he began to plan.

Centuries of experience in strategy would provide Mark with all he needed to bring her to him. After all, it worked in his business, bringing him more wealth than any man needed in one lifetime. But one lifetime's worth of wealth could never be enough for a man with unlimited life. It was why he worked so hard, that and boredom. Work had kept him busy, kept him from noticing his loneliness. Until tonight, at this moment, he hadn't realized how lonely he'd become. He'd managed to put all that behind him long ago, when she had disappeared without a trace.

He glanced again at the screen, noting her graceful neck, high, pert breasts, and long blue-jean clad legs. The clothing was different, but everything about her brought forth a familiar hunger. It was raw and needy.

"Soon, my love. Soon I'll have you in my arms again. And this time, I won't let you go."

Mark walked away toward the master suite of his family home. His footsteps might have echoed off the floor had he been like other men. Instead, barely a whisper could be heard as this large and lethal man quickly left the study. There was much to do, and he didn't wish to waste a single moment of time. Funny, he thought, all I have is time!

Meghan Hartley sat on the edge of her bed and surveyed her new domicile for the next year. Signing up as an exchange student in Romania had been the greatest decision of her life so far. In exchange for her dormitory style room and a year's worth of tuition to further her education, she would teach one class on conversational English per semester. She would attend her own classes in the morning and teach class in the afternoon five days a week. It was a great deal to handle, but well worth it. On the weekends, she would explore Bucharest and experience the Romanian culture firsthand.

Her family had asked her why in the world she wanted to go to Romania. She didn't have a concrete answer to their query. She only knew that from the first moment she studied Eastern European history, she had been fascinated by the culture of Romania. She'd always thought of herself as something of a gypsy, a free-spirited wanderer, and the lure of their mystical, bohemian lifestyle called to her blood. As far as she knew, she had never stepped foot onto this land, but here she was, as if summoned. From the first moment she stepped off the plane, she felt as if she'd come home.

A giggle burst from her lips, and she smiled, looking around the room and out her window. The old architecture of the university and the surrounding city seemed to welcome her.

"I can't wait to get out and see you," she said, staring across the quadrant to the busy streets beyond.

Meghan hummed to herself as she continued to put away her clothes. Her blonde hair bounced around her face in large curls. In the way, as usual, she thought, pushing it back over her shoulders. When the task was complete, she selected clean pajamas, and walked into her bathroom.

The room contained an old, white claw-foot tub with a shower handle mounted on the wall. Thinking a soak would be nice after that long flight, Meghan turned on the faucet and waited until the temperature was just right. She dropped the plug into the drain and let the warm water fill the tub. The sun sank below the horizon as she stripped off her travel clothes and stepped in.

"This feels nice," she murmured.

Meghan sat down carefully, letting the warm water envelop her in its heat. Laying back, she stretched out as far as she could to submerge her body and ease the stiffness in her muscles left over from the long flight. Steam fogged up the mirror above the sink. The white subway tiles gleamed in the fluorescent lighting. Outside, the last rays of sunlight faded away leaving only darkness in its wake.

To the northeast, he awakened, eyes flying open. A slow smile spread over his lips and a tingling sensation thrummed throughout his body. He felt like a live wire flowing with electricity. She's here, he thought. I can feel her.

Mark arose, muscles bunching and rippling on his naked frame. He still slept nude, a habit from his long-dead humanity. If the mirror by his bed could hold his reflection, it would reveal the hardened body of a warrior complete with a light trail of black chest hair leading a teasing path downwards, a backside that looked as if sculpted from marble, and the handsome visage of a Greek God.

Donning his clothing with precision, Marku Andrei Anghelescu made his way out of his family estate. The night beckoned him, embraced him, and then swallowed him whole as he disappeared from sight. The hunt was on, but first, he must slake his thirst before indulging the desire that burned within him.

"Mihaela, I'm coming for you."

Inside the small bathroom in the university dormitory, Meghan's skin puckered, suddenly cold. Goose flesh covered her body and she wondered at the sudden chill. Lifting her washcloth, she grabbed her body wash and began to bathe, sliding the cloth over her neck, then her breasts, and down to her belly, soothing away all her tension. It was a simple bath, but her first in this country that called to something within her heart. She smiled and completed her ablutions before stepping out of the tub to dry off. As she dried her body, a single thought filled her mind. Her life, as she knew it, was about to change.

Chapter 2

Dreams of a wild and foreign nature plagued Meghan's rest. She tossed and turned in the twin bed of her dorm room. She was standing in the middle of a vast courtyard in the dead of night. A tall man stood in front of her. She could sense the menace of his intent. She searched for his face, but it remained in shadows. He lifted his arm reaching out his hand to grab her. The grip was painful. Fingers slid around her neck, choking, and then he lifted her up over his shoulder carrying her off. Terror seized her and tried to fight back, but her body would not respond. In her mind, a single thought formed. *'He must come! Surely he would find her. Please, God!'*

A black mist shifted the dynamics of the dream and she was alone in a glade, one she knew as she'd somehow determined she'd grown up not far from it. It was evening, the sun barely peeking over the horizon, about to disappear altogether. The last rays of warmth ebbed away and a chill tip-toed over her skin.

Meghan realized she was naked. Looking down, she wondered where her clothes had gone, and why she was alone.

A twig cracked behind her. Whirling around, she searched the brush for the intruder. He stepped out, tall, dark, handsome, and dangerous. A smile spread across her lips. *"It's you!"* she said. *"Where have you been? You've been gone so long that I thought you were dead!"*

He said nothing, only walked steadily toward her, a wicked gleam in his eyes. They glowed a strange amber, in a face mostly hidden in shadows, and seemed to burn into her soul. His tread was as quiet as a panther stalking its prey. A shiver of a different kind stole over her skin. He looked... hungry.

When at last he stood before her, Meghan reached to slide her arms around his neck. He stopped her midway, grasping her wrists and lifting them above her head. He glanced down at her upturned breasts, her nipples hard from excitement and the chill of the night air, and spun her around facing away from his gaze. He kept his hands locked on her wrists, crossing her arms over her ribcage and yanking her back against the solid wall of muscles of his chest and abdomen. She moaned.

With slow deliberation, He leaned down, nuzzling her neck through the thick strands of her hair. *"Please!"* she begged. And he obliged. He held both her wrists in one of his large hands so he could lift her hair away from the warmth of her neck. Barely whispering his lips across her sensitive skin from the soft lobe of her ear down to the spot where her shoulder began, he teased her. Excitement increased the heat rising off of her body. Her salty-sweet aroma ignited the beast within. Flicking his tongue out, he tasted her.

The look of ecstasy on his face went unnoticed by Meghan who was tightly held to this magnificent man. Something hard and insistent rubbed against her backside and she pressed further back, her body seeking closer communion.

He could no longer resist her sweet temptation. Wrapping both his arms around her soft frame, he leaned in, an unholy light shining in his dark eyes. She felt this was the moment. *He'll take me now. Yes! He'll take me now.* Her body both clenched and swelled in womanly anticipation.

A low, animalistic growl escaped his lips. He was holding her too tight! *"Marku, I can't breathe,"* she said, suddenly frantic.

He squeezed tighter.

She began to struggle, to try and break his hold. Her panic only excited him further. *"You are mine,"* he said, laughing low. She turned her head to look at him, catching the bone white gleam of a sharp fang seconds before it plunged into her neck!

Meghan awoke on a half-choked scream!

She sat up slowly, hands around her neck. Her heart pounded as she searched the dim room. There was nothing to see. The moonlight shined through a crack in the curtain over her window. A breeze rippled the fabric. Meghan blinked, startled.

She didn't remember leaving that window open.

Slowly she rose and walked on tiptoes to the billowing curtains. Carefully, she lifted the edge of the material. The window was cracked open a bit as if the old-fashioned latch had come loose. She refastened it, tested it for security, then backed away to her bed. She sat there momentarily trying to recall the dream. It faded quickly away on soft gray wisps. After a few moments, she couldn't recall it at all.

She lay back down, pulling her comforter over her. In minutes, she was asleep. Meghan turned her head dreamily into the pillow, exposing two tiny pinpricks in her neck. As she slept on, they disappeared leaving only a vague, pinkish pucker.

The first full day in Bucharest was a very busy day for Meghan. She had two classes in the morning, and had to prepare for her first afternoon class teaching English over a light lunch of fruit and cheese. It was exciting, to say the least.

The crisp autumn air didn't bite, but rather, nibbled through her sweater. A breeze whipped leaves of many colors around her landing on the grass creating a beautiful patchwork covering. The old architecture surrounding the quad where she sat alone at a stone picnic table captured her imagination. A dreamy smile graced her full lips.

Today, she wore charcoal gray slacks, black boots, and a dark, hunter green sweater. She'd elected to leave her hair down to keep her neck warm although wearing it up might have added a little more maturity to her appearance. *Oh well,* she thought. *Too late now. It is what it is.*

Students of all ages walked by, going here and there. One young man played an acoustic guitar while sitting under a tree. Three girls gathered around him, listening, giggling, and goofing around. The young man seemed to be eating up all the female attention.

"Excuse me. You're Meghan Hartley?" Meghan turned quickly, startled. A tall blond man stood next to her. He wore his long hair pulled back in a ponytail.

"Yes?" she replied.

"Sorry to scare you," he said, his English heavy with a Romanian accent. "I'm Peter Petrescu, Professor of Sociology." He held out his hand to her.

"Oh. Nice to meet you. How did you know who I was?" she asked. Meghan hesitated, then shook his hand. His touch was cold, as was the metal that made contact with her skin. She glanced down and saw a heavy gold ring inset with a ruby on his pinky. It was somewhat delicate for a man's ring, but she never cared for rings on men's hands either way outside of a wedding band.

"Everyone on faculty knows who you and your friends are. A few of the professors will be attending your English class to polish up on their language skills."

He looked at her with unnerving intensity, like he was studying a bug under a microscope. His long nose and gaunt cheeks were framed by a strong jawline. His brown eyes were set deep under heavy blond brows. His height gave an illusion to his physical size which, under closer scrutiny, was muscular, not thin. He'd struck her as long and lean at first until he moved his wide shoulders in a shrug.

"Well," she said, "that's a little intimidating knowing I'll be teaching tenured instructors. Now, I'm really nervous."

"Don't be. You'll be fine. So how are you settling in? Everything to your liking? No bad experiences so far?" He fired off the questions in rapid succession. It was weird. He seemed to be staring a hole through her.

"Everything is fine so far, thank you."

He stared a half second longer before pulling himself up to his full height. "Then I'll leave you to your planning. It was good to meet you, Miss Hartley." With that, he reached for her hand, lifted it, and kissed her fingers like a throwback to another time.

"Nice to meet you, too," she replied, yanking her hand back. His lips on her skin felt revolting. She couldn't explain why she took such an instant dislike to this man if she tried.

He noticed her response and cocked his head, his brow furrowed. Then, Petrescu smiled and turned to leave. "I shall be seeing you around," he said as he walked away.

She hoped not. He was creepy. How could such a creepy man be a professor of sociology? She shivered as if someone had danced over her grave. She crossed herself like her grandmother used to do.

Trying to forget that meeting, Meghan went back to her lesson plan. Today was going to be a good day, and no creepy stranger was going to spoil it for her.

Her first class was a success. Meghan had a total of twenty-four students, ten of whom were faculty who were trying to better their English. Everyone had been courteous and eager. She started off by stating the class would be a total emersion into English. Only English would be spoken during class time. Meghan had taken two years' worth of courses of the Romanian language and could hold a simple conversation, so if anyone faltered, she could help get them back on track.

She spent half the class speaking their language before starting to work in baby steps toward basic English. It had been great fun.

One of her new students was a woman named Dana Veleru. Dana was one of the mathematics professors. Short, dark-haired, and round, she had an open and expressive face. Meghan liked her straight off.

"So, you are liking it here in Bucharest so far, yes?" said Dana with a big smile. Her English was a little better than most having taken a year of study three years prior. "My apology if my English is not so good. I have no one to practice with me."

"Your English is good, Dana. I understand you just fine," said Meghan.

"Ah, good." Dana clapped her hands. "We will be greatest friends, you and me. You will see. Come, let us go to get drinks and you can tell me about you, and I can tell you about me."

Meghan couldn't resist the enthusiasm from her new friend. They were around the same age with Dana being maybe three years older. She wasn't one-hundred percent sure, but she figured she was about to find out. Dana seemed like an open, and chatty, book.

"Okay. One drink! Only one. I'm not sure I can handle more than that."

"Ha! No one drink only one drink in Romania! Would be insult to host." Dana linked her arm through Meghan's and led her up the cobbled street.

From the street, Peter Petrescu watched the twosome leave. He scowled. Anyone looking would have seen the slight down-turn of his lips at the edges, but no one paid him any mind. He opened the door to his car and sat inside.

To the east, storm clouds gathered, slowly blotting out the sun. The dull gray sky turned dusky, a bad omen.

Petrescu glanced up at the impending darkness. "I know you are out there somewhere," he whispered. "But I found her first, and this time, she's mine."

Lightning flashed across the sky followed by a low, angry rumble of thunder. For a moment, Peter was shaken, as if he hadn't expected such a dramatic reply. Then he tilted his head back and laughed. "Come and try," he said. "Come and try."

The engine roared to life, and he pulled out of the parking lot, driving in the direction he last saw the two women walking. Rain began to fall, striking the stone cobbles with force. Puddles filled in the cracks quickly as people caught in the sudden downpour ran, dashing for cover.

The sun, hidden behind the angry clouds, had nearly set when the two laughing and wet women tumbled into the door of the tavern. Shaking her head, Meghan looked around the interior of the small room. Dana shrugged out of her coat and encouraged Meghan to do the same.

"You will warm up faster this way," she said.

Meghan's eyes took in the neat rows of tables along the far wall. Two wooden booths looked out over the front facing window. Red tablecloths covered every table and each had a candle set inside a glass globe in the center creating a warm and inviting ambience. The bar stood along the back wall. It was old and pitted from years of use. A rack of glasses and bottles were lined up behind it. All the bottles looked old, like the kind you might find on a movie set depicting an ancient European tavern. The lighting was dim, but a fireplace in the corner gave off a soft glow.

"It's charming," Meghan said as she folded her coat over her arm.

"My cousin owns it. His wife makes the best soup in town. It will warm you from inside out." Dana grabbed Meghan's hand and led her to one of the booths.

The place was nearly full. A few people had trickled in after them and found seats at the bar. Men and women lifted glasses to make toasts, talking and laughing with great animation.

A short woman approached, a big smile on her face. "Dana, you bring me new customer!" The woman leaned over to give Dana a hug.

"Meghan Hartley, this is Ilana, my cousin's wife. Ilana, this is new American English teacher at university." Dana's smile matched that of Ilana's.

"Welcome, Meghan!" Ilana grabbed Meghan up in a big, friendly hug. Apparently, no one was spared the warm family greeting.

"You must be chilled. I bring you both hot soup and bread. I just took from oven before you come in." Ilana patted Meghan on the shoulder and walked quickly away with purposeful strides toward a back door that led to the kitchen.

"She's very nice, your cousin's wife. Her English is pretty good. I'm surprised."

"Oh, she lived many years in Germany before coming back here and marrying Stefan. She gave him so hard time. He chase after her for nearly one year before she consent to a marriage!" Dana's hands gestured, punctuating her story.

"She really had him panting after her then?" Meghan asked.

"Yes! It was laughing to see," Dana said, chuckling.

"Funny. It was funny to see." Meghan corrected her automatically.

"Yes, yes, that too!"

Ilana interrupted at that moment placing two steaming bowls of soup in front of the women. A tall man standing behind her carried a platter containing a warm loaf of bread, some cheese slices, and grapes.

"This my husband, Stefan." Ilana put her arm around the tall man's waist and propelled him forward.

"Salut." Stefan's deep voice greeted her. He had long features; a long face, long nose, long, lanky frame. His eyes were big and dark, and fringed with long lashes. They were very pretty eyes for a man, and they twinkled with mischief. Right away, Meghan could see that Stefan was a kind man because kindness radiated from his eyes, so very like his cousin's.

"He not speak any English, Meghan," stated Ilana. She took the platter of bread and cheese from his hands and put it on the table.

"That's okay. I speak Romanian as well," she said, switching to their native tongue.

It was then Meghan noticed a boy, a smaller version of Stefan, around the age of ten, coming up behind the couple with a flask and two glasses.

"Is that your son?" asked Meghan, speaking Romanian.

"Yes! Yes, this is Alexandru. You speak Romanian! She speaks Romanian!" said Stefan with great excitement, gesturing to Ilana and Dana.

Dana rolled her eyes at her cousin, giving him a look that said, *"Of course, she does!"*

"Idiot! Meghan is educated woman, not typical American tourist." Dana and her cousin began speaking rapidly in their native language with her gesticulating at him, and he obviously baiting her so she would get more frazzled. Anyone could see these two had been around each other since birth. Stefan seemed to laugh with his eyes more and more, and Dana became more annoyed with him by the minute. Finally, she realized he was teasing her and burst out laughing.

"Fool! Why do I always fall for your foolishness?" She lifted her spoon while Ilana took both glasses and began to fill them with red wine.

"Because he is the devil himself and tempts you to anger with his wickedness!" Ilana elbowed Stefan while she spoke.

"Ouch, woman!" He feigned injury for a moment before wrapping both arms around his wife's waist. "I will expect apologies for your abuse later, my tiny doll." This last was spoken almost too low for Meghan to hear. However, Ilana heard it and blushed knowing exactly what Stefan meant.

Dana and Meghan exchanged knowing grins before tucking into the savory beef and vegetable soup. It was as delicious as her new friend had said it would be.

"Is good, yes?' asked Ilana, already knowing the answer by the ecstatic look on Meghan's face. "I leave you two to enjoy meal. I come check on you in short time."

"Ya, Ilana. Go and give Stefan a stern lecture about annoying me," said Dana between mouthfuls of soup.

Ilana left the women to their meal.

It was an incredibly delicious, down-home meal. Meghan sampled a crusty piece of warm bread. She added a slice of cheese on top and took big bites, her eyes closing as the flavors teased her tongue. This was why it was called comfort food. Nearly an hour later, she was full, and felt warm and fuzzy from the good meal and even better wine. As Dana had said, she did not stop at one glass. It was too flavorful. It would have been like trying to stop at one potato chip after fasting. In this moment, all was right in the world. She sighed, content.

Their candle sputtered and danced on a cold breeze as the door to the tavern swung inward. Meghan turned her head to see the source of the chill creeping over her skin and locked eyes with the most beautiful man she had ever seen.

The door closed leaving the entryway in silhouette, but she could still see the outline of a chiseled face surveying the room. She couldn't see his eyes anymore, but she had an odd sense he was staring at her. Her face warmed.

The momentary hush that fell over the establishment began to pick up pace again as people turned back to their companions to continue conversations. The man walked out of the shad-ows and into the glow given off by the fire. He wore a long, dark leather trench coat. Meghan couldn't tell if it was brown or black in the dim light. It looked expensive though. Below the hem of the coat she saw dark slacks and expensive-looking leather shoes. Her eyes came back up again to stare at his face, noticing the shine of his dark hair. It looked almost black in the dim interior, but the firelight picked up on the rich caramel strands. He wore it long and tied back in a leather thong. She could see it was wavy and her fingers flexed with a desire to delve into his thick mane.

The man walked over to a corner table and sat with his back against the wall. He shrugged out of the trench coat letting it fall over the back of the seat. His eyes surveyed the room and all within it as he made himself comfortable. Meghan turned back to her friend but found herself peeking at him from the corner of her eye. She knew the moment his gaze lit upon her because it felt like a physical touch.

Dana continued to talk, but she, too, had noticed the man. Reaching for the silver cross that rested around her neck, she said a silent prayer. In Romania, there were stories of the "dark ones". She'd grown up on them. Never once, though, had she believed her grandmother when she spun her tales to a young girl at bedtime. They were just stories, after all. Her grandmother was a direct descendant of a gypsy clan that came from the mountains in Moldova. She told young Dana that gypsy blood flowed through her, even if it was watered down by the weaker Hungarian blood of her father. Grandmother never approved of her daughter's choice of husband. *"You will know the truth of my stories one day, little one," she had said. "When you come into the presence of one of the dark ones, you will feel it deep inside, like being on fire from within." Her warning seemed so dire, Dana had giggled. 'Silence!" said Grandmama. "When you feel this fire, run! Your life will depend on it."*

It had been nearly twenty years since Dana last heard that vehement warning spoken in the night by the light of a candle, and she had chalked it up to good theater. Gypsies were known for being dramatic. Now, as a fire built within her bosom, she knew the truth of those words. The man who walked in and sat down, the man with a face like an angel, was one of the dark ones. Everything inside her screamed, *"Run!"* She felt both silly and terrified at the same time.

Dana noticed that Meghan had locked eyes with the man, and that the man was staring at her friend. She also knew the moment his eyes slid to her. The fire inside her turned suddenly cold. She heard a deep voice in her head sneer, *"Gypsy"*.

Dana startled and turned her now frightened eyes in his direction. For one split second their gazes locked. In that moment, he smiled at her, and she knew she must do as her grandmama had bid her to do all those years ago. *Run!*

"Meghan, we should go now. I have early class." Meghan jerked her head around at Dana's words. Her tone had changed from happy and jovial to clipped and stern. She wondered momentarily if she had accidentally missed something her friend had said while she was checking out the hunky man and inadvertently offended her.

"Sorry, did I miss something?" she asked.

"No. It is later than I first realized. Really, we must go now!" Dana tried to keep her words light so as not to alarm Meghan that anything was wrong, but something in her dark eyes told a different story.

She rose out of the booth, grabbing her coat and sliding her arms into the sleeves. Then Dana helped a slower Meghan slip into her own coat. Ilana approached after noticing the two women preparing to leave.

"Leaving so soon, cousin?" she smiled, unaware of Dana's urgency.

"Ya, Ilana. How much do I owe you for dinner?" Dana asked while reaching inside her purse for her wallet.

Meghan, too, had reached inside her own purse to retrieve money for her half of the bill.

Ilana patted both women's hands. "No, not necessary. You are family. No pay usually, but as it happens..."

"I have bought your dinner for you. I hope you don't mind." Meghan turned at the sound of this new, deep and vibrant voice. The man, the one with an angel's face, smiled down at her with such rugged beauty she almost forgot to breathe.

"Thank you." Meghan stumbled over her words, embarrassed.

"My pleasure," he said, taking Meghan's hand and bestowing the lightest touch of his lips on the back of her knuckles. She felt the strangest sensation of electricity tingling where those lips had touched her skin.

"It's not every day I encounter so much loveliness. Perhaps I could persuade you ladies to stay and have one drink with me before you leave?" His eyes gleamed at Meghan who blushed behind her smile. Then, he slid his penetrating, dark gaze over at Dana, staring down into her terrified eyes. "What say you?" *Gypsy.*

That last word was never spoken aloud, but Dana heard it as clear as a bell tolling a death knell. A quick side glance at her companion showed Dana she had not moved fast enough. Meghan was staring at this dark creature as if he were the most charming, most handsome man on the planet. Dana knew she had failed her grandmother by not believing her all those winters past. This man was, indeed, one of the dark ones, and he wanted Meghan, just as sure as the sun rose and set. He also knew that Dana knew what he was. He knew what she was as well, a gypsy descendant. It might be too late, but she would not let him have her friend. The gypsy people were loyal if nothing else.

"So sorry, but we must go. Thank you for dinner." Before Meghan could say a word, Dana grabbed her hand and pulled her to the door.

"Dana!" said Meghan, sending an apologetic look over her shoulder at the beautiful man.

He smiled slowly, and bowed his head in her direction, never losing eye contact. Before she was pulled completely out of the door, he winked at her, and her heart fluttered wildly in her chest.

"Another time," he said. Meghan shrugged before the tavern door closed, cutting him off from her sight.

Dana marched quickly back toward campus where she was determined to deposit Meghan safely in her room. She knew now she would need to go see her grandmother tonight. There was no time to waste. As the wind howled, and stray drops of rain smacked the cobbles of the street, she could hear the faint laughter of the dark one inside her head.

Chapter 3

Mark stood watching the tavern door slowly closing, cutting off his view of Meghan. The feelings simmering inside him threatened to boil over. He struggled to clamp them down. Feelings. He hadn't experienced this chaos within himself for almost eight hundred years. *How did I ever stand this before?* The look of interest in her eyes invited him in, and he wanted to be closer. He wanted to be as close as a man could get to a woman, within her, tasting her, swallowing her essence. And by now he would be if it weren't for that damn gypsy woman!

He hadn't counted on that. The familiar smell of gypsy blood given off by the short, smiling woman had surprised Mark. He didn't encounter this particular tribe anymore. In fact, it had been sixty years since he last scented Curarya blood. She must be a descendant.

The Curarya clan once roamed freely, and in great numbers in his homeland of Moldova. Mihaela's people had come from a branch of the Curarya, the Lovarya. Because of this, Mihaela was not even a consideration for marriage to one such as himself. The Anghelescu's were of noble blood, and Marku was destined for great things including aligning his family to even greater fortune through marriage to the daughter of one of his father's greatest friends, Count Latcu cel Mare. Marku Anghelescu had never met his intended bride to be. He had never made it to that day alive.

One year earlier, as he rode into the village near his home of castle Anghelescu, he had come upon a scene that changed his life. There, in the middle of the dirt road, a beautiful woman with honey-colored hair was throwing rocks at a tall, blond man. She missed more than she hit, but when one of her missiles connected, it connected with strength!

She was yelling at the man, who continued to try and corner her. A crowd had gathered, creating a semi-circle around the melee. The man stalked her until her back was to the village well. She had nowhere left to run.

"I will not marry you, Peter! I do not care what our fathers say!" She screamed at him, anger and fear in her voice.

"Mihaela, you have no choice in this matter. You will do as your father says and we will be married tomorrow. Then you will be mine!" The tall man sneered at his cornered bride-to-be.

The terror on her face said more than her words ever could. She didn't just have a dislike of her father's choice of husband, she was afraid of him. Something in Marku sparked to life. He never liked to see a woman abused. His own mother was a saint with the kindest heart in the world. She not only cared for her family, but she also put herself forward to offer care to the sick and the infirmed of their people. No child, elderly, or animal went without a kind word or basket of food and supplies either made or put together by his mother's own hands.

This woman was desperate. The man continued to approach her, a choice he would regret.

Feeling behind her, Mihaela found the ledge of the well. "Do not come any closer! I will jump down this well if you do!" Grasping the edge, she sat herself upon it, swinging one leg over.

"If you attempt to jump, I will make sure you wish you were successful!" said Peter. He was within arms-length of her now.

She spat in his face.

"You will be sorry for that!" With lightning speed, Peter swung out with his right hand, slapping the young woman so hard that she stumbled and fell sideways off the ledge.

Sprawled on the ground, she hid her face with her hands, trying in vain to hide the tears and the shame.

This was the moment that changed his life. Marku snapped.

"Stop!" He pulled his sword, rushing forth, and forced the blond man back and away from the girl. With the tip pointed at the man's chest, Marku put himself between the two.

"This is not your concern," Peter stated, anger and venom in every word. "She is mine!"

"I heard her say different, mongrel!" The two men eyed each other. "And everything that goes on here is my concern. This is my land," said Marku.

"An Anghelescu," Peter replied with derision. "You think you can interfere in Curarya business just because you live in a great house? We are the Rom! We follow no law but our own, the Zakono!"

"Filthy gypsy dog! Your law holds no power in my realm. I can kill you here and now, and no one would stop me. But it is your lucky day. I'm prepared to let you leave with your head intact. The terms of my leniency are simple; get off my land and never return!" Marku touched the tip of his sword to Peter's neck. The man glared at him, his eyes filled with hate.

Peter knew he would have to comply, despite the urge to fight. He was not armed, and did not have any backup with him. He had chased Mihaela into town on foot after she ran from his advances earlier in the day. He'd had every intention of branding her as his own although the wedding was set for the next day. He would not let her get away from him. He'd waited too long and had been spurned by her too often since their fathers had made the wedding pact.

Retreat was the only way at this moment. Anghelescu was right. This was his realm. All the Curarya knew it. They traveled through here every spring under peaceful agreement with this cur's father. Peter's father would not be pleased if his actions today upset the rhythms of their clan.

Backing up, Peter kept his eyes on Mihaela. "I will see you at home, Mihaela. Be assured that I will be waiting with both our fathers when you return." With that, he turned and walked east out of the village toward the clearing where their family had set up camp.

Marku slowly lowered, then sheathed his sword. He turned to look down at the woman. She had remained on the ground behind his legs during the entire altercation. Looking up at him now, she felt her heart expand in her chest. He'd saved her from yet another beating at the hands of that monster. For three years Mihaela had sought every way to get out of her marriage pact to Peter. She knew all along what a cruel person he was. She'd seen him fly arrows into his younger brother's pet dog for fun, killing the animal slowly. She'd witnessed him kicking an old man in the last village where they'd set up camp. The old man had done nothing to deserve such treatment. Peter was simply an evil man who derived pleasure from causing pain.

When their fathers had agreed to a marriage contract, she'd nearly fainted in horror. Her family was poorer than most, but Peter's family had offered what would be considered a fortune for her hand in marriage. This was not common practice, but Mihaela was no common young woman. Among her people, she was considered exceptionally beautiful.

Peter had grown up around her, but never noticed her beauty until she had suddenly blossomed one summer. A fire burned within him when he gazed upon her. He would have her and no other. He'd gone to his father that day and demanded that he arrange a marriage contract between their two families. His father had laughed until he saw the seriousness in his son's eyes.

The first meeting between their families did not produce an agreement. Mihaela had refused to accept Peter, and being a man who loved his daughter, Simion had refused on her behalf. Peter did not give up. The next night, he and his father had returned, demanding that Simion align with their family. Peter's father, Janus, had not taken the rejection well, either. He had a puffed up sense of himself and his importance within the clan. As he saw it, any family would be honored to be allied with his. The two patriarchs clashed verbally, and five meetings later, with much bargaining and veiled threats exchanged, an agreement had been reached. The only major stipulation had been that Mihaela be allowed to grow into her full womanhood before she wed. After all, at the time she was only fourteen years old. It was the last gift of goodwill from her father, the best he could do considering that his greed in upping his status in the clan had made him barter his daughter's happiness.

She was given a reprieve of three years. In those three years, Peter had tried time and again to bed her, beating her when she refused his advances. No one helped her. All her people turned a blind eye to the bruises. Until today.

The man standing before her had done what no one else had. He'd protected her. And he was handsome! His dark curls framed a strong face with warm dark eyes. His lips were full, his shoulders broad, and his height equaled that of Peter's. But where Peter was tall and lean, this man was muscular. His body was evidence of a warrior's training.

Marku smiled down at the vision of loveliness sitting at his feet. Her large brown eyes had impossibly long lashes, and their almond shape drew him in to their velvety depths. Her skin was like fine cream kissed by the sun, and her full lips seemed ready to burst with ripeness. Not to be outdone, her lush bosom pushed forth over the top of her blouse cinched close to her waist by her corset. He extended his hand, and she shyly placed her own smaller one in his. The electricity that shot through his entire being at that innocent touch had left its mark upon him. From that day forward, he knew she would be his.

In the distance, the scene was observed by jealous eyes. As anger burned in his heart, Peter slipped away, unseen, into the darkness of the forest.

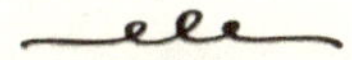

Peter Petrescu watched the woman walk quickly away from the cluster of dormitories. Dana Veleru seemed to be talking to herself. She looked upset as she made the sign of the cross and hurried across the quad in haste to catch the last bus for the night.

He glanced up at the window where a light came on. A shapely silhouette passed out of sight before returning to pull the blind down. He imagined she would now be getting undressed and ready for sleep. The thought of her laying in her bed stirred his blood. He easily recalled her long legs, full bosom, and lush lips. His fingers twitched at his sides, itching to sink into her blonde tresses. He wanted to dominate her, to hold her down and claim her as his own. But he knew he must control himself. Lack of control would ruin his plans. He was going to have to play it cool, woo her. He had a clean slate now, and he was not going to take any chances. This time, she would be his. He just needed to be what she wanted—a charming gentleman. Petrescu lit a thin cigarette and took a long drag. After centuries, he'd learned patience. He would exercise that ability now. He walked back to his car planning his next move. As he slid into the driver's seat, he noticed that the light in her room was now off. "Sleep, Mihaela, for tomorrow, our courtship begins."

Chapter 4

"I'm sorry I didn't believe you." Dana marched through the open door past the old woman who stood holding it open with a surprised look on her face. That look was quickly replaced by a somber wisdom.

"You've seen one," she said, closing the door and blocking the cold, damp wind. The old woman peeked out the window before pulling the shade closed.

"Yes." Dana turned and looked at her grandmother.

"And you ran?" She hobbled slowly to the stuffed chair by the wood-burning stove and sat, adjusting herself until she was comfortable. She pointed a crooked finger at the chair opposite. Dana took the seat, but remained on the edge, still very much ill at ease.

"Not fast enough." She shrugged out of her coat and pulled it onto her lap like a protective shield.

"Why do you say this? What happened?"

"He was after Meghan, and would have had her had I not pulled her away."

The glow from the grate in the old iron stove cast shadows about the room. Normally, it felt cozy, but tonight, the shadows seemed to hold deep, dark secrets. The low light emphasized the lines in her grandmother's face, and Dana was surprised by how many there appeared to be. She didn't usually notice them as her grandmother was most often smiling, but she was not smiling now, and the seriousness of her countenance increased the fear in her heart.

"Who is this Meghan?"

"She is an exchange student come from America. She is also teaching English. We went to Ilana and Stefan's for dinner. That is where I saw the dark one."

"Go on. How did you know?" The old woman sat forward, waiting.

Dana's eyes reflected her terror. "It was just like you said all those years ago. When he came in, I felt a fire burn inside of me like nothing I have experienced. It was both burning hot and ice cold. I just knew in that moment I must get out of there, but he already had her attention. And that's not the worst part, grandmama."

"Tell me, child."

"He knew me." Dana's voice lowered to a whisper as if speaking any louder might alert the devil to her whereabouts.

"He knew... what?" Her grandmother's eyes pierced hers.

"He spoke..." She struggled to explain. "He spoke, but only I could hear him. He called me... *gypsy!*"

The old woman gasped, and immediately made the sign of the cross before spitting over her left shoulder twice. "You are sure?"

"Yes, he did it not once, but twice."

"Dearest lord, he is truly a dark one." Worry marred her grandmother's face. She sat back and stared into the fiery grate, quietly considering what she'd just learned. Finally, she turned to her granddaughter. "But you got away? He did not chase you?"

Dana shook her head. "No. I made sure we got away. I made sure to get Meghan to her room, and then I came here. I need to know what to do, grandmama. What do I do?"

"That is most strange," she said. "And this Meghan, how did she react to the dark one? You said he had her attention?"

"She noticed him noticing her. Actually, he paid for our dinner." Dana raised an eyebrow at the strangeness of that statement. "But he seemed focused on her, and I think I was just in the way."

"He wants her. He was warning you to not interfere, and you interfered." The harshness in her rebuke made Dana jump.

"Was I supposed to just let him have her? She is my friend. I could not leave her."

Her grandmother continued to glare at her, and then wrinkle by wrinkle, her angry expression smoothed out. "No, of course not. You are gypsy, so you are loyal to a fault. But hear me, Dana.

He has warned you of his intent. He will not offer warning again. You must not cross his path."

"I was not looking to cross paths with this dark one at all, but I need to know what to do. How can I protect Meghan?"

The old woman sighed. "You will have to be very sneaky."

"Why?" Dana looked confused.

"Because, you foolish girl, she will not believe you. She is not from here. Americans think dark ones are fantasy from movies and books. Your friend knows not of the Curarya ways. She is not gypsy. You will have to be smart about this."

"But how?"

"A charm, to start. I will help you, but we must act fast. I need to collect the necessary items. We are going to make a protective talisman for your friend. You will present it to her as gift, but she must never take it off while she is here. It will be up to you to make sure she wears it." The old woman leaned forward once again. "We will extend the Curarya clan's protection to this young woman, Dana, but you must remember that she is an outsider, and if this dark one comes for her anyway, if my magic is not strong enough to keep her safe, then you must save yourself!"

Meghan awoke feeling refreshed. Today, she had two classes of her own before teaching in the afternoon. After a quick bath, she dressed, wrapped a red scarf around her neck, slipped into her coat, and grabbed her books before heading out to the cafeteria. She was quite fond of having her coffee in the morning. It helped her wake up and got her energized. Outside, light flakes of snow fell, slowly covering the ground. It made the pathway slippery, but she managed to make it to the cafeteria door without falling. It was warm inside, and the scents of bread, eggs, and coffee lifted her spirit. She headed for the line, picking up a tray along with utensils. Three students were ahead of her trying to decide between wheat and rye rolls, and poached versus American-styled scrambled eggs. Meghan picked up a coffee mug and slowly pushed her tray down the line choosing the scrambled eggs and whole wheat roll with what appeared to be authentically churned butter.

"A hearty breakfast, I see."

Meghan jumped. The deeply accented voice coming from behind immediately filled her with dread. She didn't understand why, but when she turned around, the blond professor from the day before was standing there, a little too close for her personal comfort.

"Sorry, you startled me. Mr. Petrescu, wasn't it?" She tried to step away and leave a little more space between them.

"Peter, please." He smiled and pushed his own tray closer once again. "And how was your first day?"

Meghan came to the coffee pots where she reached for one of the glass pitchers. Petrescu was faster and grabbed the handle first while taking her mug from her hand and pouring the steaming brew up to the rim. He handed it back, but something in Meghan hesitated. Feeling silly, she took the now full cup and when his fingers touched hers, she cringed. A feeling worse than the dread caused by his voice shot through her, and she suddenly wanted to run.

"Thank you." She set the cup on the tray, sure now that she would not drink it. "It was fine. Thanks for asking." She arrived at the cashier and paid for her breakfast. Desperate to get away from this man who set off all her alarm bells, she turned. "Well, gotta run. I have class in twenty minutes and need to hurry."

"Then I guess I'll see you this afternoon." He smiled.

Meghan stopped, confused. "This afternoon?"

"Yes, I'll be joining your English class. Just to brush up, of course."

Pasting a weak smile on her face, she nodded. "I'm not sure you'll get much out of it. Your English is already very good. Are you sure you wouldn't benefit from one of the other more advanced courses?"

"Not at all. I'm sure you will be just fine for my needs." His dark eyes seemed to be saying something else entirely and it was creeping Meghan out.

"My class," she said.

"What?" He blinked.

"My class. My class will be fine for your needs. Not me." She corrected him hoping that was what he meant.

"Ah, yes. See? It is the smallest nuances. Thank you for my first lesson." He gave a sort-of mocking bow, his smile more of a smirk now.

"Okay, well, see you later." Meghan didn't want the conversation to go on any longer. She quickly ended it and made her way to the far side of the cafeteria where she dumped the food into the trash, all except for her roll which she carried with her as she walked outside into the cold. All she wanted to do was get away—fast.

Petrescu watched her go, a speculative glint in his dark eyes.

Outside, Meghan shook off the bad feelings the man inspired in her. She couldn't pinpoint a single thing he'd done to cause her to feel the way she did, but her mother always taught her to trust her instincts, and her instincts screamed at her that this guy was bad news. She decided to keep her guard up and maintain a comfortable distance from Petrescu, but having him in her class was going to make the rest of the semester miserable on that score. Hopefully, with all the other students and Dana there, she wouldn't notice so much. Meghan was glad to have made a friend who would help distract from anything negative.

Dana sat through Meghan's English class, but with a touch of impatience. She clutched a small box in her sweater pocket, turning it over and over again while she recited common English phrases along with the other students.

"Where is the bathroom?" Meghan said.

"Where is the bathroom?" The class repeated after her.

"How much does it cost?" Meghan walked back and forth in front of the class.

"How much does it cost?" they all replied.

"Good. In America, you will find that there are many ways people say hello. Some of those ways are, "Hello, Hi, Hey, What's up? How's it hangin'? Yo!, How are you doing?" She smiled at their confused faces. "I know. It can be difficult. Often when someone asks you how you're doing, they don't actually want to know how you're doing. They're really just saying hello."

"Then why not just say hello?"

Meghan saw Peter Petrescu raising his hand while simultaneously speaking. Her smile fell. "That's a great question. It's more of a regional colloquialism. Certain areas of the country use very particular phrases. For example, in the south, a lot of people speak with a drawl," she lapsed into her best *Gone with The Wind* Scarlett O'Hara impression, "and they say 'ya'll' instead of you or you all. In those southern states, they will ask, 'How're ya'll doin'?' instead of 'How are you doing?' whereas up in New York," she switched to Joey Tribbiani from *Friends*, "a person might say, 'How you doin'?' It depends upon what area of the U.S. you happen to be in. That's probably pretty confusing, but if you stick with the tried and true, just say *hello* and *how are you* for those you don't know, and *hi, hey,* and *what's up* for those you do know. That would be your formal and informal greetings."

Dana raised her hand.

"Yes, Ms. Veleru?" Meghan acknowledged her formally.

"What means this, *'What is up?'* I do not understand how this means hello."

Meghan laughed low. "It's like asking someone what's going on or what's new since last I saw you. Does that help?"

Dana nodded.

"Does everyone understand, or do you have any questions?" Meghan addressed the class.

Everyone nodded yes, but a few seemed unsure.

"It's okay if you don't quite get it yet. We'll be going over it all again tomorrow when you come to class. The first thing I want everyone to do then is to greet your fellow classmates with any of the phrases I introduced today, okay?"

"Okay," they replied, nodding their heads.

"Okay, then I will see you all tomorrow. Same time. Same classroom." She waved as they all got up to leave.

Meghan walked to her desk to retrieve her purse and books. When she turned around, Petrescu was right behind her.

"Oh, my gosh! You scared me." She tried to step back and away, but the desk blocked her.

He stood tall, looming over her. A half-smile curled the edges of his thin lips. "My apologies. I did not mean to." He continued standing in her personal space.

"You wanted something?" Meghan composed herself, trying not to appear unsettled by his odd behavior.

He stared into her eyes, which began to creep her out. "I was wondering if perhaps you might like to join me for coffee."

His invitation caught her off guard, and as she searched her brain for a polite way to refuse him, another voice interrupted.

"Meghan, you are ready to go?" Dana stepped in, taking her hand and leading her around Petrescu.

"I am, Dana." Meghan turned to him. "I'm sorry, I have plans. See you in class." She let Dana pull her out the door. When they were halfway down the hall, Meghan grabbed her new friend and hugged her. "Thank you!"

Dana shrugged. "It is nothing. I see you did not want his advances. I don't know why he is even in your class. He speaks better English than all of us. Strange man." She muttered the last, but Meghan heard only the words spoken before that.

"I thought so, too. What in the world is he doing taking my class?" She spoke the words out loud.

"It is obvious. He is, as you say in America, into you. But if you ask me, he is big creep." They walked out into the cold air. It was late afternoon, and the sun was already beginning its descent.

"Ew, Dana. I don't want him to be 'into' me. I agree he's a creep, but why do you think so? Has he ever said or done anything to you?"

The shorter woman shook her head no. "I cannot put finger on it, but there is something not right about him. There is no soul in his eyes. It is as if he is dead person who still walks around." She crossed herself.

"That's a weird thing to say. But I think I agree." Meghan felt a prickling sensation and looked back over her shoulder.

Petrescu exited the building and stopped. His eyes caught hers across the quad and his expression looked almost angry before a small smile spread across his face. He gave her a jaunty wave. Meghan turned back around quickly, spooked now, and wondering how to avoid the creepy Peter Petrescu for the remainder of the academic year.

Chapter 5

Mark spied them as they came through the door. He sat in the back of the tavern slowly swirling the whiskey around in his glass. He was surprised the gypsy brought her back to this place although he was pleased. She looked beautiful in the firelight. The shadows danced around her as if respecting her natural glow. He could see it in her cheeks, a blush offering a hint of pink to her creamy skin. To the casual eye, it was nothing but the cold causing her body to react with heat, but to him, it was more. He could almost hear the blood rushing through her veins. It sounded like the beckoning roar of a waterfall on a hot summer's day. Soothing, yet stirring. Even from across the room he could taste her scent on the air, a warm honey, a sweet, fragrant nectar, one he remembered even now. Mark Anghelescu knew now that the blood that ran through his Mihaela then now flowed through the heart of Meghan Hartley. He licked his lips recalling the smallest taste of her only a few nights past.

Neither woman noticed him. He stayed in the shadows, with several tables in between, observing. The tavern owners came out and approached their table. Their greeting was familiar, the women known to them. He could see a hint of resemblance between the gypsy woman and the tall man who owned the place. He could even detect his gypsy blood, although it was not as strong as hers. Family. Curarya.

The owners left them alone with drinks and food. Meghan spoke with great animation while the little gypsy listened, her body not quite relaxed. His love ate the food placed before her, and her companion pulled something out of her pocket. She set it on the table and pushed it toward Meghan, who looked surprised. The gypsy smiled and indicated Meghan should open the small box. She did.

As he watched, she pulled a silver locket out and held it up to the light. The fire caught the metal illuminating the markings on the round disc. His keen vision clearly saw the symbolic etchings in the silver. He also detected it contained iron and a hint of sawdust, which surely was hidden within. The runic writing contained three words in ancient Romany; Death to Strigoi. And he was the Strigoi in question. It was a ward, a fetish, a talisman crafted by an old witch, one who he suspected was an older relation to the little gypsy. Power pulsed from the object in Meghan's hands, although he knew she had no clue.

The small one stood and helped to place it around her neck. Then Meghan stood, hugging her friend. The gypsy had given his love a locket of protection—against him. The anger that bubbled inside him swelled to the surface, but he exercised control and clamped it down. Only moments ago, he felt almost conciliatory toward the gypsy, but now he knew he would have to kill her, and the gypsy witch who created the talisman. The first because she meddled in his business, and the second because only her death would break the spell on the necklace that now hung around Meghan's smooth, supple neck.

He stood gathering his leather duster coat around him and, moving faster than the human eye could detect, exited the tavern. Those sitting at the bar looked up as a sharp gust of wind ruffled the hairs on the backs of their necks, and a few glanced back at the tavern door that seemed to open and close on its own accord, setting the candles to flickering.

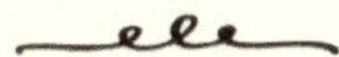

Dana stared with wide eyes as the door to the tavern swiftly opened, and now slowly closed. The strong gust of wind that blew out the candle on their table chilled her cheeks. She looked around, but saw nothing else amiss. Still, she crossed herself, asking the Blessed Virgin to protect her.

"I can't believe you, Dana. This is so beautiful. It must be very old." Meghan looked down at the locket hanging around her neck admiring the etchings. "What does it say?"

Dana remembered to smile, and then picked up her fork waving off Meghan's words.

"I'm glad you like it. I found it at a gypsy market. Just a trinket. Gypsies are famous for selling off their junk, not that it is junk," she said quickly, laughing, "but still, I saw it and thought of you. It is a friendship locket. The words, I am not completely sure, but they are a sort of protection, a prayer for your well-being. You should wear it always while you are here in Romania. It will keep you safe." Her tone was much more serious when speaking these last words.

"Well, I'm certainly not superstitious, but I am sentimental, and this is my first gift from my new friend." Meghan reached out and took Dana's hand. "Thank you so much. I just love it." She gave her fingers an affectionate squeeze. "Do you think it will help keep that creepy professor away?"

Dana laughed. "If it doesn't, I will squash him for you like bug. No worries."

Meghan took another bite of her stew. She savored the spices and the warm gravy while looking around the tavern. "I wonder what ever happened to that other one?"

Dana kept her eyes down on her fork. She knew to whom Meghan referred but didn't want to entertain that train of thought. She slipped into her native tongue. "Who knows? Lots of people come through here. We will find you a nice Romanian man if you want. I have many single cousyns. You must come to my home and meet the family this weekend. It is my grand-mama's birthday. She will be eighty-one."

"Wow! That's wonderful. Are you sure? I'd hate to be in the way—" Meghan was both excited and yet not willing to crash a family event uninvited.

"You will not be in the way. You are my friend. I am inviting you. Ilana and Stefan will be there, so you already know someone else besides me, and my family is very big, very welcoming. You will have a good time. Lots of food, good wine, good friends, and dancing!" She grinned.

It all sounded too good to be true. Meghan was excited by the prospect of experiencing authentic Romanian culture, and also about being with friends. She was used to her family back home, and she missed them. The Velerus might just help heal the homesickness in her heart.

"Okay. I would be honored to come."

"Very good! I will pick you up on Saturday. Pack for the weekend. You will be staying with me." Dana pulled off a chunk of bread and ate it.

"Pack? I thought it was just a birthday party." Her eyes grew wide.

"Yes, yes, but it is Romanian birthday party, and we celebrate all day and all night. Then we rest and begin again. You will enjoy it so much. The Rom never do small parties." She sipped her wine.

"The Rom? Your family are gypsies?" The smile spread across Meghan's lips.

"Of course. The Curarya. Did I not say?" She laughed.

"No, missy, you didn't, but now I'm even more excited."

"Just you wait, Meghan. It will be the time of your life!"

After a good meal, better wine, and excellent conversation, Meghan returned to her dormitory. As she slipped upstairs to her room, a shadow grew out of the darkness and stepped into the light of the moon. He stood there, watching her window as the light came on, and waited until it dimmed once again.

Mark could not believe what he was seeing. From the top of the Humanities building, across from Meghan's dorm room, he waited. When he saw her return and climb the stairs to her floor, he'd planned to wait until she slept before visiting her room as he did the first night she arrived. But his keen eyes caught movement on the ground below. A tall man stepped out from beneath the canopy of trees. He stood staring up at the same window that Mark watched. As the clouds slid across the moon, the silvery light shone down upon him illuminating the blond hair. When the man turned to gaze up at the second floor window, Mark saw his face clearly. It was a face he had not seen in eight hundred years, one he assumed had faded to dust long ago.

"Petrescu!"

He shook himself. It just couldn't be the same man, the one he long suspected had a hand in the disappearance of Mihaela. If it was him, how had he obtained immortality? His senses did not reveal anything preternatural about him. In fact, he smelled blood. The man was human. Was he also a reincarnation of the gypsy dog Petrescu? While it would seem incredible, it was entirely possible. The irony was not lost on Mark as he considered the idea that somehow, all three of them were cosmically linked, with himself as the only one who knew why. Still, he should have killed Peter Pretrescu when he had the chance. Had he done so, Mihaela might have lived out her life with him as planned, but there was a flaw in that theory. Marku Anghelescu, the man he was then, had never arrived the night they planned to run away together.

That very evening before his marriage to the daughter of Count Latcu cel Mare, his father's greatest friend, he rode out with only the most necessary items and a purse full of money to meet Mihaela in the glen where they first made love. The moon was high that night, and although his heart was heavy with the betrayal to his parents, it was also filled with love for the woman of his choosing, the woman he loved above all others. When he arrived, Mihaela was not there. He'd ridden straight for the gypsy camp with murder in mind for her jilted fiancé.

Marku knew that her father, Simion, would help him find Peter. He'd paid dearly enough to the swindler for the right to break her engagement to Petrescu and have her as his own, but the others in camp might not be so cooperative to the nobleman's son. Even though it was his family's land they camped upon each spring, they respected no one but their own elders, and they viewed Anghelescu as an outsider. Getting answers and finding the coward was not easy, and more than one eye had to be blackened before Marku located him.

The gypsy dog said he knew nothing, but dared to laugh at him saying he hoped whoever had her, had her every which way they could so she would be ruined. Then he spit at Marku's feet. A red haze blazed before his eyes and he leapt upon the man, beating him down. Petrescu gave as good as he got, and the fight was on. In no time, the entire camp surrounded them cheering their own on. When each was bruised and bloodied, Simion stepped forth and shouted, "Cease!"

It was then the old man spoke, berating them both for selfishly fighting while his daughter was missing. He rallied the camp and they set out to find her. Several took to their horses to follow the trail left in the glen while Marku had to return to his home, black and blue, and heavy of heart. He charged Simion with letting him know as soon as they found her. In the meantime, he knew he had to tell his parents he could not marry Alexandra. It was the right thing to do even though it came late, and at a price.

But his parents would have none of it. They insisted he forget the gypsy girl, and that he proceed with the wedding as planned. His father, Dragos, gave him no choice.

"This alliance cannot be broken!" He railed at his son. "The joining of the houses of Anghelescu and Cel Mare is important for the political future of Romania, and you will not destroy all I have built, all that Count Latcu has built because you cannot control your cock!" Dragos slammed his hand down on his desk, his dark brows furrowed fiercely over his black eyes. "If you must have this trollop, then keep her as your mistress, but you will do so discreetly. I will not have you dishonoring Alexandra, do you hear me, Marku?" The man stood to his full height which topped his son by two inches, and pointed his finger, shaking it with resolve.

Marku straightened his back, and looked his father in the eye. He knew he could not refuse him, not now. He gave the briefest nod of his head in acknowledgement.

"Good. Now go upstairs and let your mother tend to those cuts. You will remain in the castle until the ceremony tomorrow night." Dragos dismissed his son.

Marku retreated to his room and allowed his mother to fuss over him. When she left, he leaned out his window, staring off into the night. To the east, he could see the light in the distance from torches at the Curarya camp. His heart was full of worry for Mihaela. He needed to know what happened to her, where she was. He needed to explain to her about the change in their plans, but he didn't know how. He would honor his parents, but he needed to make sure she was not harmed, that she was safe.

He waited several hours for the household to quiet, and for his parents to go to bed. Once the moon had reached its zenith, he crept downstairs and out the side door to the stables. He would simply go to the camp and see if there was any news. If they needed help, he would help. If he must ride out, he would ride out, but he would return in time to do what was expected so as not to dishonor his parents and the House of Anghelescu. That was his plan. Simple. But plans often do not proceed accordingly. Often, they spin out of control and have deadly consequences.

Mark came back to the present leaving his thoughts in the past. He watched the man watching Meghan.

"So, fate has brought me a second chance. Apparently, you think you have one, too, Petrescu," he whispered to himself. "It seems I have the advantage of knowing the outcome this time." Mark shifted his attention, and instead of visiting Meghan while she dreamed, he moved as silent as the night, following the second coming of Peter Petrescu home.

Chapter 6

The car pulled into the driveway, heading for the garage. The door went up after he clicked the button on the remote, and Petrescu drove his Audi inside. The red brick house with the steepled roof sat at the end of Strada Romulus not far from the university. The crumbling mortar between the bricks showed the home's age, but it also displayed character. With two floors and an attic, it provided Peter with more than enough room to putter around in between classes. He turned off the motor and stepped out, reaching in to grab his briefcase. A chill crept over his skin, and he straightened, scanning the yard beyond the interior of the garage.

The darkness of the night obscured his sight for the most part, but the streetlamp offered some light. Nothing moved, but that fact did not seem to reassure the prickling at the back of his neck. He closed the car door and set his briefcase on the roof of the vehicle. Petrescu took three steps toward the open driveway.

He stood there scanning the shadows in his overgrown yard. His ears sought any hint of sound, and his eyes focused, seeking the slightest movement. The air was still. The usual sounds of the night seemed to have ceased altogether. A slow smile began to creep across his thin lips. He ducked back inside the garage and picked up his briefcase. As he approached the three steps that led to the kitchen door, he looked out one last time before he flipped the switch on the wall. The garage door descended, its metallic gears grinding and filling the silence. A soft thud sounded as it hit the floor and silence once again reigned. He went inside, closing and locking the door behind him.

Outside, a shadow disengaged from the rock wall along the sidewalk. It swiftly grew, and then moved quietly up the side of the house, coming to rest upon an eave overlooking one of the second-floor windows. From there, Mark Anghelescu observed as lights came on inside the rooms on the first floor. His preternatural hearing picked up the sound of footsteps upon the stairs. They walked to a room where they paused, shuffled, and then approached the window upon where he perched. Mark looked down as light filtered through the curtains. From his vantage, he could not see the man inside, but when he popped the latch and slid the window open, Mark leaned out over the eave just a bit. When the man poked his blond head through, looking out over the dark yard, Anghelescu's fangs elongated, and an unholy light cast an amber glow in his black eyes. Closer than he'd been before, he could smell the blood pumping through the Petrescu lookalike's veins. It smelled familiar.

Mark's brow furrowed as he tried to place where he'd encountered this scent before. The odor of it set off a reaction, one created by memory. He inhaled deeply allowing the scent to settle upon his tongue, tasting it.

He froze.

It cannot be! The memory was strong and could not be denied. The man leaning out of the window beneath his reach was Peter Petrescu. Not a reincarnation, not a descendant, but the man himself!

Petrescu disappeared back inside the window. He closed the sash and locked it once again.

Mark hissed low, "What witchcraft is this?" He knew the man was not an immortal like himself. He would sense it, and there would be no heart pumping, no blood running through his veins. For him to still be alive after eight hundred years was not possible. But the scent of a person does not lie. Each human had their own individual and unique flavor. It could not be duplicated, not in descendants or doppelgangers. It might be similar, but there were always variations, thus individuality. Even reincarnations were different. His Meghan had much of the earthy honey of Mihaela, but she also had her own fresh scent. Pear-like, crisp and sweet. Mihaela was more apple and mossy woods.

If this truly was the Lovarya gypsy who cost him Mihaela, then he not only needed to protect Meghan from him, he also had a very old score to settle.

Carefully, he descended along the side of the house where he'd come up, then stood in the yard staring up at the window. Without an invitation, he could not get inside to kill the man. Mark would have to bide his time, but first, he needed to plant a seed. He left, returning to the student dormitory. Entering this building was easy since it was public property. He found Meghan's room and listened through the door. He could hear her soft breathing. The steady rhythm told him she was now sound asleep. He slowly dissolved into smoke and slipped beneath the door. On the other side, he solidified.

He could smell the iron and sawdust inside the locket. It was an old Romany safeguard against vampires, one that on its own, did nothing, but blessed by a powerful gypsy witch, effectively warded the Strigoi, and could even kill them should they come into contact with the talisman. The glint of metal caught his eye and Mark saw that Meghan had taken the necklace off and left it sitting on the nightstand by her bed. He was sure he remembered the little gypsy telling her she must wear it at all times for protection, but she did not tell her why. And being American, Meghan did not take such superstitions seriously. A point in his favor. *This will make things much easier,* he thought. *I may not have to kill her friend after all.*

Mark sat on the edge of her bed gazing upon her beauty. Reaching out, he touched her face letting his fingers caress her cheek. One finger skimmed down to her mouth. He ran the pad of his thumb softly over the fullness of her lower lip. Meghan sighed, shifting slightly. Resting his hand upon her smooth, bare neck, Mark entered her dreams.

The glen was dark, but the moon was high. Meghan knew this place. It felt familiar and comforting. The soft whoosh of water running through the river behind her filled her with peace. She was lying upon the soft grass staring up at the stars. A rustling in the rushes caught her attention, and when she turned her head to see what it was, her heart began to pound. He was here!

Tall, muscular, and powerful, he strode across the grass approaching her with the grace of a mountain lion. Shadows hid his eyes, but she detected the smile upon his lips. Happiness filled her although she couldn't understand why. She both knew, and didn't know this man. Her mind questioned his identity, but both her body and heart welcomed him. He stopped and stood over her, blocking the light from the moon.

"I have missed you." The warmth of his words filled her with joy. The husky edge to his deep voice sent shivers down her spine.

"I know you," she said. Meghan began to sit up, but he dropped down, leaning over her and bringing his face within inches of her own. He had both hands on the ground on either side of her head, and he slowly covered her body with his own, sliding a knee between her thighs and urging them open.

"It has been too long, Mihaela." He whispered her name as his hips fit themselves snuggly into the vee of her womanhood.

Meghan opened her mouth to ask who 'Mihaela' was, but she was silenced by his kiss. It began softly, wearing her down with each petal-soft caress. His hot lips infused her entire being with tingling warmth. She sighed and his tongue swooped in, tasting her, deepening the kiss. Desire flooded her body as she felt his growing need pressing into her, and rubbing back and forth against the thin barrier of her nightgown.

Nightgown?

She couldn't make heads or tails out of what was happening, but she knew it was one sexy dream. She played along.

Boldly, she raised her hips to meet his thrusts as his mouth left hers to lick a hot path to her ear, and down her neck to her shoulder. She ran her hands up his bare arms, feeling the muscles. They were like steel beneath his skin. He moaned, and the sound made her feel powerful.

When his fingers moved to unbutton her gown, she arched her back. His deft hands spread the material wide exposing her breasts to the chill of the night air. Her nipples puckered and he sucked in a breath.

"Magnificent! I have missed your taste, my love." Before she could respond, his hands slid up capturing each breast, massaging them while he stared in rapture at the bounty he beheld. His fingers kneaded, then lightly pinched her nipples before he descended and took first one, and then the other into his mouth, sucking greedily.

Meghan groaned her pleasure. My God, this is the best dream ever! She was eager to see it to its conclusion as need rose within her.

"You are mine. Say it!" He whispered fiercely between nibbles and licks of his tongue.

"I'm yours," Meghan replied, eyes closed as he trailed kisses further down her taut belly and lower still. Before she could even whimper, he plunged his tongue deep into her moist core causing her to shout, "Yes! Oh, yes!"

Her fingers slid into his thick hair and gripped the strands tight. He expertly licked and sucked, tweaking her sensitive nub with quick flicks of his tongue while his hands held her hips in his strong grip. Meghan knew she was close to climax.

"Oh, God. Yes! Please!" She begged him for more.

"Please what, my love?" His deep tone vibrated against her.

She could tell he was smiling, enjoying having her right where he wanted her.

"Please, please, don't stop!" She arched her back trying to lift her hips, but he had her well under control.

"Don't stop what? This?" He gave her a long lick.

"Oh, yes!" Sweat beaded along her brow.

"Or this," he inquired as he sucked her nub hard, flicking it with his tongue.

"Oh, oh!" Meghan thought she would just die if he didn't stop teasing her.

He laughed low, and then began working her in earnest. Each thrust of his tongue sent her higher, and one large hand reached up and gently squeezed her breast, pinching her nipple while his mouth worked its magic. The pleasure/pain took her over the edge, and Meghan's body exploded in a wondrous orgasm that made her thighs quiver.

As she tried to catch her breath, marveling at the realism of her dream, her dream lover rose up, pushed down his pants, and revealed his massive rod. It bobbed in the breeze only for a moment as he reached down to guide himself to her wet and willing opening. Meghan couldn't believe her luck and vivid imagination, but she gladly spread her knees wide and allowed him to inch inside filling her. It took her breath away.

"Sweet God, I cannot believe you are here." The reverence in his voice thrilled her. She reached to pull him closer, and as their lips met, he pushed hard, thrusting home.

Their bodies knew each other, recognized each other's needs. They began a dance as old as time, and as she wrapped her legs around his waist, he rode her hard. He pushed up on his arms, his back arched, muscles bulging in his chest, shoulders, and biceps. Meghan could only stare at him in awe. The moon came out from behind the clouds shedding its light upon them. His face was illuminated at last. She could see the strong jaw, full lips, high cheekbones, and she was dumbstruck by his raw male beauty. Then he opened his eyes.

They glowed amber.

"What! Hey, what—" Fear welled up from the pit of her stomach, and when he smiled, bone-white fangs peeked out of the

corners of his lips. She opened her mouth to scream, but it was too late.

He thrust hard one last time, then swooped down, sinking those sharp teeth into her neck.

Meghan braced for the pain, but instead, felt only mind-blowing ecstasy wash over her. As her body shuddered, the dream began to fall apart. Before he disappeared, she heard him whisper in her ear, "Beware of Petrescu. He is coming for you."

Her eyes popped open, and Meghan sat up in her bed, clutching her neck. She reached for the spot where he'd bitten her in the dream and found nothing. But her heart pounded with fear. She was dripping with sweat from head to toe. She looked around her room. All was quiet. All was still. And she still felt the dull, throbbing ache between her legs.

Chapter 7

Friday arrived on a blustery wind. The skies were gray all day, the clouds filled with the promise of rain, but that didn't seem to dampen Dana's enthusiasm. She jumped out of the large blue Volkswagon van that looked like a throwback to the early seventies. There were actually curtains hanging in the windows pulled back by beaded ties in every hue imaginable. Stefan was in the driver's seat, and Ilana sat next to him. Meghan laughed.

"I can see this is going to be an adventure." She eyed the interior as she approached. Dana hugged her and took her duffel bag that was packed with enough clothes to get through the weekend along with her toiletries.

"You just wait and see, Meghan. You're going to have so much fun; you will never leave. Which is okay by me. I will adopt you as my sister and you can change your name to Veleru!"

"I think my mother would have a hurt feeling or two about that. So would my dad." She grinned.

"Well, maybe you can marry one of my brothers or cousins then, and your parents will be over the moon to see you become part of such a nice family." Dana placed Meghan's bag in the very back of the van. Meghan pulled out her cell phone and insisted they take a selfie. She made sure to get the crazy van curtains in the background.

"Say cheese!" Meghan aimed the eye of the camera in her phone at them. Dana grinned, and the flash went off. The girls giggled while Stefan sighed at their antics, clearly ready to leave. Meghan clicked to add it to her page. She was still typing up the post as she settled inside on the bench seat. Dana climbed in, taking the seat next to her, and sliding the side door shut.

"Ha! Your brothers." Stefan hooted, speaking in his native tongue. "Sorin is too much the ladies' man for Meghan, and Cosmin is too much a sour puss, and already married. That one, Meghan," he looked back at her in the rearview mirror, "is never happy. Always going on about the Romanian government, politics, conservatism and returning to the old ways, yada yada yada. I'm sure he was switched at birth and really belongs to a New Republic power couple and not the Curarya." He stopped at the end of the road, checking both ways before turning right and heading out of the city through Old Town.

"He's not that bad, Stefan." Ilana patted his shoulder and turned to Meghan. "Now, our cousin, Fabian, he's a good one. Just about your age, and an engineer!" She said the last with great emphasis. "He's also considered very handsome by the local girls, but he will not make it home this weekend."

Meghan stifled a giggle. These crazy, warm, and wonderful gypsies would have her married off before the end of the weekend and popping out babies by Christmas if she let them have their way. Her thoughts strayed to the dreams she'd experienced this past week. Each night since the first one, she'd dreamt of the same man. Marku. In each dream, he made love to her passionately, satisfying her in ways she'd never experienced in reality, not that she'd had much experience. There was Troy, her first, but they'd dated only two months the summer before her senior year in high school. And then there was David, her first college boyfriend. He made her freshmen year wonderful, but as it turned out, he also made Shelly Anderson's freshmen year 'wonderful' too. His cheating ended their romance. She'd been single since, and now Meghan was haunted by a dream lover who seemed to know her body better than she did. And strangely, he would often bite her neck which had her thinking she'd read one too many vampire novels. But the strangest part of all was the warnings. Each time he left her, he told her to beware of Peter Petrescu. That's what bothered her the most. It was one thing for her subconscious to invent a dream lover, she was fine with that. It was quite another thing to ruin it all with dire warnings about a creepy professor she already knew to steer clear of. Her instincts had told her from the beginning something was off about him. She didn't know what, exactly, but she had no intention of ever finding out. He was still in her class, but she could keep him at a distance by maintaining her professionalism. She avoided him easily by leaving right away at the end of class. Dana helped a lot, and she was grateful. Other than that, she hadn't run into him on campus the entire week. Still, the nocturnal messages didn't sit well with her.

Meghan had thought about telling Dana about them, but she didn't know how to even bring it up, and she didn't want to share the juicy bits. Maybe a little distraction from fantasy land would be good for her.

"I'm sure he is. Especially if he has the family eyelashes." Meghan leaned up to tease Stefan, speaking in Romanian. "Why is it the boys always get the prettiest eyelashes?"

Ilana laughed. She knew Stefan got embarrassed whenever anyone remarked upon his eyes. To her surprise, he batted them like a Hollywood starlet and replied, "I couldn't say, but I know they helped to lure this one in." He reached out to grab Ilana's hand. She blushed bright red at his show of affection.

Meghan smiled as she looked at the woman. Her long, dark hair was thick and full, falling nearly to her waist. As tiny as she was, she looked like a doll with her pink cheeks and red, bow-shaped lips.

"Where's Alexandru?" she asked, inquiring after their son.

"He is already at the compound. Sorin came and helped Stefan fix a leak in our roof yesterday, and he took him along when he left this morning. Alexandru loves his grandmother, and he was so eager to get there to see all his cousins too."

"A compound? How big is this house?" Meghan turned to Dana who was bouncing in her seat with every bump in the road that Stefan hit.

"It is huge, Meghan. There are four acres of land, three houses sit on those acres, and many smaller cabins near the river."

"Holy cow! It sounds like a resort." She hoped that she'd brought appropriate clothing. Most of what she packed was casual.

"No, no. It is family home, that's all. You will love it. You will stay in the main house with me. I have two beds in my room. Stefan and Ilana will stay in their cabin. You will see. The Curarya take very good care of their own."

Stefan chimed in. "The land has been in our family for so many generations, no one can say for sure how far back that ownership goes, but grandfather used to tell us stories about how our people worked the land every year when they traveled through. Most still travel and only come to stay during the summer and for special occasions. You can't ever completely remove the need to wander from a gypsy."

"And the ones that stay?" Meghan asked.

"Cosmin and his wife, Anamaria, they are always there with grandmother since grandfather passed. My mother and aunt, Stefan's mother, they also live there in the other two houses. The family grows corn, wheat, potatoes, and we also have a modest crop of grapes, mostly for the wine!" Dana grinned.

"Your family makes its own wine? Well, this really is going to be an adventure then." Meghan was impressed.

They spent the rest of the ride out of town filling Meghan in on everyone she would meet. The gypsy van rolled through the streets of Old Town, and then finally arrived at the outskirts. Stefan turned onto a stretch of country road leading toward the mountains in the distance. Very few vehicles took that exit, but a dark colored Audi lagged several cars behind.

Mark's eyes opened as soon as the sun went down. He lay still surrounded by the red velvet drapes that framed his canopy bed. They were more ornamental than anything since the windows in his room were covered by steel shutters set on a timer. In another minute they would slide on their perfectly greased rails to reveal the moon rising in the night sky. It was one of the few modern luxuries he had installed in his family home, that and an elaborate security system, and WiFi for his computer. He felt strange. Something was off this evening. His senses told him everything inside his room and his house were the same. Nothing amiss. But he felt off. He reached out with his preternatural psychic abilities, *feeling* around for whatever was wrong. As his mind wandered in concentric circles steadily reaching out and away from his home, it hit him. He didn't feel Meghan, couldn't sense her.

Mark sat up quickly, his mind racing in a beeline for her dorm room. Ever since he'd begun visiting her nightly in her dreams, he'd been building a psychic bond with her. One where he could easily locate her whereabouts, sense her moods, and even know when she was thinking about him. Of course, to Meghan, he was still just a dream lover that satisfied her body in every erotic way possible, but to him, each moment strengthened his own feelings for her, merging not only his body to hers, but his mind, heart, and whatever was left of his soul. Those moments also fed the demon that lived inside of him. He didn't need to actually drink her blood to feed off her. Psychic energy was just as good, if not better, than blood although the taste of her on his tongue was its own pleasure.

"Where have you gone, Meghan?" He jumped out of bed and rushed to his closet. Inside, he chose black jeans, a black cashmere sweater, and black snakeskin boots. He dressed quickly while mentally searching the areas around Old Town where the university was located. He could not find her, and if she was nowhere to be found, only one person could possibly be to blame.

"Petrescu!"

He spat the name out even as he was already plotting the man's murder.

Mark ran his fingers through his hair as he thought. He went straight to his computer. Meghan was a normal American college student. If she was going to share her whereabouts anywhere, it would be on her social media. He sat in his chair spinning around to the desk where his fingers flew across the keyboard pulling up her MySpot account. He'd neglected checking in on her since he'd been invading her dreams. His time with her there lulled him into a sort of complacency, but he figured if she was making plans, she would have told him while they were in their glen.

He smirked. "Well, when did I give her any chance to think of other things?" he said out loud.

He knew he spent most of their midnight moments kissing her breathless, nibbling away her cares, caressing her skin, licking her senseless, and pounding her most sensitive flesh with his own. The only other time words were spoken happened when he left her with the warning to beware of Petrescu.

Her page came up, flashing a picture of her with the little gypsy woman standing outside of a van. The caption read, *"My first gypsy care-a-van! On my way to celebrate my friend's grandmother's birthday."* Dana Veleru was tagged in the image and now Mark knew the meddling gypsy's name.

He opened a new tab and looked up Veleru. There were many. However, it wasn't so much the names he was interested in, but their locations. He found that the largest concentration of Velerus were located south from his own home, about two miles, and sitting upon land that once belonged to his family. He knew the area well. Very well. A slow smile spread across his face.

"So, Meghan, the time has come." He shut down the computer and picked up his cell phone. Although he eschewed most technology, he found he rather liked the convenience of GPS mapping, checking his business email, and one guilty pleasure he would never admit, playing Candy Crush. He was up into the six hundred thousandth level. He was willing to bet most people didn't even know it went that high. He had a lot of time on his hands, and until recently, not much to do with it outside of business deals.

Mark walked out of the house, setting the alarm as he went. He headed straight for the stables. Tonight, he would use a more conventional mode of travel. As he approached, Dracula whinnied, then stomped the ground. Mark still found it humorous that he'd named the black stallion after the very man who inspired the myth of vampires. At least, the world believed it to be a myth. He knew otherwise, and so did every gypsy born into the life of a traveler. The stories were passed down verbally from generation to generation. The young ones these days usually thought they were just that, stories. But those who encountered the Strigoi, crossed their paths on a dark night, soon knew the truth to every single tale told around a campfire.

Dana Veleru knew the truth now. And he figured her taking Meghan out of the city was her way of keeping his woman from him. Little did she realize how futile the effort, that nothing would keep him from claiming Meghan. She was his, had always been his, and fate brought her to him. He would not let her get away a second time. Dracula snorted, impatient to run. Mark tightened the straps of the leather saddle and mounted the massive steed.

"Are you ready, my friend?" He gripped the reigns, letting the majestic animal know who was in control.

Dracula threw back his head, snorted loudly, expelling puffs of air visible on the cool breeze, and danced in place eager to get moving.

Mark laughed. "Good. Then let's go get our woman!" He dug his heels into the stallion's sides and Dracula took off in a full run heading for the open field. Rider and beast were soon swallowed up into the night.

Chapter 8

Meghan was overwhelmed. There were so many people; aunts, uncles, cousins, brothers, sisters, nieces, nephews, parents, and one very energetic grandmother. Dana pulled Meghan's hand as she led her to the center of all the people standing outside of the main house. Near the fire pit, an old woman stood wearing a dark gray sweater paired with a long, ruby-red skirt over black boots. Her slate-colored hair was piled atop her head in a messy bun, and her face was both open and full of character. She smiled as Dana approached revealing a missing tooth on the upper right side. Although small in stature, she exuded a powerful presence.

"Grandmama, this is my friend, Meghan Hartley." Dana stepped next to the old woman and put her arm around her. "And Meghan, this is my grandmama, Adina Lazar Veleru."

Meghan extended her hand. The old woman clasped it between her own. Her hands felt warm and strong despite her frail build. Her wrinkled skin looked paper-thin, and the joints of her fingers were twisted with arthritis, but the comfort in her touch was undeniable.

"Happy birthday, Mrs. Veleru." Meghan smiled down at the woman, then her smile slipped a notch as she noticed the intense expression transforming the old woman's face.

Adina gripped Meghan's hand tighter, and then she flipped it over, extending the younger woman's fingers. She stared at her palm, and one gnarled digit traced the lines she found there.

"Sweet Virgin, we are too late!" She glanced up at Meghan and then cast a wide-eyed look at her granddaughter. "The necklace, you gave it to her?" Adina Veleru looked back at Meghan, her eyes searching around her neck. There, hanging just beneath her sweater was the necklace she'd helped Dana fashion, the one infused with her magic. "You have it on now, but you've removed it, yes?" She looked up at Meghan, accusation in her tone.

Meghan's free hand flew to her neck and she gripped the chain hanging there. "Well, sometimes. Like when I take a bath and go to sleep. Why? What's this about? Are you doing some kind of palm reading thing?" She half-smiled, but the uncertainty in her voice showed she wasn't sure how to respond.

Dana looked at her friend. She blinked and cast her eyes down, turning back to her grandmother. "I tried, grandmama, but I didn't quite know how to explain it without Meghan thinking we were crazy." Tears welled in her eyes. "I've failed her, haven't I? I failed my friend. I failed you. I'm so sorry, grandmama. Meghan." She reached out, laying her hand over the one her grandmother still clasped.

"I don't understand—" Meghan began.

"Of course, you don't! You are not Curarya, not gypsy! But I will explain it to you, and you had better heed my words, Meghan Hartley, for they may be the only thing that might save you now." She tugged Meghan's hand and pulled her over to the chairs around the fire. "Sit."

Meghan chose a red lawn chair and Dana pulled one up next to her. She sat, and then reached over to take her friend's hand. She held it tight offering a look of apology in her now sad brown eyes.

The old woman sat down opposite the two girls in an old rust-colored recliner that had been placed outside for her comfort. She sat with her spine straight and shoulders back, regal as a queen. Her eyes held Meghan's, staring beyond the physical into her soul.

"When my granddaughter came to me last week, I was alarmed. I have never seen her so distraught. I'd hoped never to see her that upset, hoped she would not ever find herself in the presence of a dark one."

The gravity of her tone left Meghan unsettled. "If I've somehow offended you...," she looked at Dana, "I'm so sorry. I had no idea. Please accept my apology."

"You did nothing, Meghan. The dark one is not you. Let grandmama explain." She patted her friend's hand.

"You are marked. I see it in your aura, and I read it in the lines of your palm. He has already marked you. You let him in, Meghan. You removed the only protection I could offer when you took off your necklace, and you allowed him a way in. You have been having dreams, yes?"

Meghan stiffened. She looked at the old woman, surprised.

"No need to answer. I see it in your eyes. He has been coming to you night after night, visiting his lust upon you, and you have received him."

The accusation was thick. Meghan felt like she was being dressed down by her father for wrongdoing. "I don't understand. I mean, yes, I've been having some really wild dreams, but they're just dreams—"

"Not just dreams! The dark one is a master manipulator. He will make you his in your mind first, and then he will come for your body. He wants you, and he will not stop until he has you." She sat forward, eyeing the young woman. "What has he said to you in these dreams?"

Meghan flushed, her cheeks burning. She wanted to lie, but found she couldn't do so to save her life. Dana gave her hand a supportive squeeze.

"He tells me he loves me. That I'm his."

Adina Veleru sucked in air and sat back. "What else?" she demanded.

Meghan looked at Dana. "He leaves me with a warning each time."

Dana blinked back the tears in her eyes. "What does he warn you about?"

"Professor Petrescu." Meghan clearly felt that this was all surreal, that it couldn't possibly be happening.

"Who is this?" Adina asked her granddaughter.

Dana turned to her with a confused expression. "He's a professor of sociology at the university. He pestered Meghan for a bit, but lately, he seems to have gotten the message she isn't interested. He's creepy, grandmama. I don't like him." She spit on the ground.

"Always trust your instincts, Dana." She addressed Meghan again. "What is your assessment of this Petrescu?"

"I don't like him. Something feels off about him, and he makes my skin crawl. I just avoid him, but he is in my English class, so I still have to see him there." Meghan shuddered.

"He approached you first?" The old woman pried.

"Yes, he came up and introduced himself to me when I first arrived."

Adina sat, thinking.

Meghan glanced at her friend. "Dana, is Petrescu supposed to be the dark one? If he is, why would my dreams warn me about him? What does this all mean?"

Dana shook her head. "No. He is big creep for sure, but he is not the dark one. The dark one you met at Stefan's and Ilana's pub."

Meghan looked thoughtful trying to remember who else she met while at the tavern. The only other person she could recall outside of Dana's family was the handsome man who bought their dinner, the one she left standing there as her friend practically pulled her out the door.

"Yes, him." Dana could see the understanding cross Meghan's face.

"But we didn't even talk to him except to refuse his offer to stay. I don't get it. What was so dark about him? He was very handsome." Something clicked in Meghan's memory. The shadows that always covered her dream lover's face were suddenly lifted, and she could see him clearly. She gasped.

"Now you see," said the old woman. "Dana knew what he was that night. He spoke to her, recognized her."

"I didn't see him speak to you..." Meghan began.

"You didn't hear him because he spoke only in my head. He called me *gypsy*. I heard him as clear as a bell." Dana shook her head, fear in her words.

"You're talking about telepathy. But that's just cra—" Meghan stopped herself from confirming her friend's fear that she thought her crazy.

"Is it?" The old woman asked. "Why is it crazy to think he could communicate with his mind when he has been seducing you in your dreams?"

Meghan flashed to each vivid dream she'd had in the past week. They had all maintained a quality unlike any dream she'd ever had before. She could feel everything, smell everything, taste...everything. She'd even climaxed in every dream, sometimes multiple times. But to entertain the idea that a man she'd seen only once in passing could be insinuating himself into her dreams would surely mean she was losing her marbles. It wasn't even possible...was it?

"What, exactly, is a dark one? You keep saying that, but what does that mean? Some kind of evil mind-reader?" Meghan waited, almost holding her breath, fearful Dana's grandmother would tell her some psycho stalker had fixated on her.

Adina stood and walked to her. She squatted down slowly, her age making it difficult, and sat upon her knees, placing her hands on Meghan's, which were sitting on her blue-jeaned thighs. "He is not of this world, child. He is far older than even myself. This man, if we can call him that, is not some smitten, unwelcomed suitor." She paused, taking a deep breath. "He is Strigoi. He is vampire."

Dana crossed herself. Meghan stopped breathing. The old woman searched her face.

Suddenly, Meghan began to laugh. It started as a nervous giggle, then flowed out uncontrollably despite trying to hold it in. She knew it was disrespectful, and she bit her lip hard to stop.

"You laugh? You think this is a game?" Adina stood to her full height and looked down upon Meghan with disapproval.

Meghan grew serious once again. "I'm sorry. I didn't mean to offend you. It's just that, well, you just told me I have a vampire dream stalker, and where I come from, that's just absurd. That sort of thing only happens in movies."

"Bah!" Adina looked at Dana. "I told you she would not believe. I warned you, and now you've placed yourself between the Strigoi and what it wants. It will surely kill you, and it will not be because I did not warn you!"

The volume of Adina's voice rose. Stefan, Cosmin, and Sorin all turned from their conversations and came closer. Ilana followed. Sorin put down the guitar he'd been playing and came up behind his grandmother placing his hands on her shoulders.

"Grandmama, why are you getting so upset? What is it?"

The old woman pointed at Meghan. "She has attracted a Strigoi and put your sister in danger. She will not listen to me. It will kill her and anyone who gets in its way!"

Sorin looked at her. He was a year younger than Meghan, but tall, fit, and as handsome as Dana had suggested on their ride up. He had black, wavy hair and startling blue eyes. He'd been all smiles when they arrived, but now his expression was dead serious.

"Is this true? Have you put my sister in danger?"

Meghan blinked, shocked that he believed in monsters and was angry. "I...I don't know." She turned her hands up. "I don't believe in these things, but if I've somehow put Dana in danger, I'm sorry. I can leave." She stood.

"Leaving will not help. It will only place you in further danger. And it doesn't matter if you don't believe in Strigoi." He held his grandmother close to his side. The old woman looked disgusted. "The Strigoi believes in you, and if it has decided it wants you, there's not a lot that will prevent it from taking you.

And Miss Hartley, just so you understand, you won't survive."
Sorin spoke better English than Dana, having spent a year attending college in London.

Meghan looked at all of them one by one. As she searched
their faces for any hint of a group joke, that hope died as
each pair of eyes reflected back the seriousness of their be-
liefs. Even Dana's parents, Marius and Renee, came to stand in
the semi-circle surrounding her. There were varying degrees of
anger and disapproval, all of which made Meghan itch to run
away.

"You really believe this," she said, more a statement than a
question. She turned to Dana who still stood by her side holding
her hand. "You really believe in vampires? So this necklace,"
she reached to pull it out from beneath her sweater, "wasn't an
antique friendship locket, but some kind of vampire repellent?"

Dana took a deep breath. "Yes. I could not think of anything
that would show you my friendship more than trying to save
your life." She looked straight into Meghan's eyes. "That night
at Stefan and Ilana's tavern, he spoke inside my head. He was
mocking me, Meghan. He knew exactly what I was, and he was
not afraid to show me this. He knew I would believe, and that
I would protect myself. What he didn't know was that I would
protect you too. He wanted you then. Wants you now. That is
why you have been having those dreams. Why didn't you tell
me?"

"Because I didn't know. I'm not like you. I wasn't raised on stories of vampires. They're just fictional characters in books and movies for me."

"All fiction comes from a kernel of truth, Meghan."

Meghan felt tears sting the backs of her eyes. "I'm sorry, Dana. I wouldn't for the world put you in danger. I can call a taxi and leave. I see that I've offended your family and I'm deeply sorry." She began pulling her hands away.

"No!" Dana held on tighter. "We do not abandon friends." She looked at her family. "Just because she did not know, does not believe, does not mean we will hand her to the Strigoi by leaving her unprotected. That is not our way." She looked at her grandmother, beseeching.

Some of the starch came out of Adina's spine. "No, you are right. It is not our way. We are loyal to those we care about." The old woman looked at Meghan. "Young lady, you may not believe in our monsters, but we do, and we will keep our promise to Dana to protect you. That is what Curarya do. You will stay," she left Sorin's side and walked to Meghan, "and you will not remove that necklace no matter what, do you understand?" She pointed a bony finger at her.

Meghan nodded, pulling herself back to gain space. She looked around at the growing circle of faces. Stefan's mother and father joined them along with Cosmin's wife, her cousin, and their siblings. The anger had retreated from their expressions and in its place was resolve. No one was going to let anything happen to her.

"There is but one thing left to do." The old woman turned and nodded at Stefan who left the group to go inside the house. She turned back. "If we are going to protect you like family, you will become family...tonight!"

"What does that mean?" Meghan asked as Dana grinned and pulled her friend over toward the fire pit.

"It is a ritual, Meghan. Tonight, you become Curarya, and from this night forward, you will always be one of us."

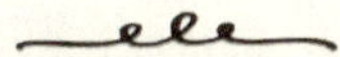

Mark pulled the reins tight, bringing Dracula to a halt. The stallion snorted, breathing hard. He was just inside the tree line of the clearing that opened out exposing three houses in the distance. Beneath the light of the moon, he could see the firelight, and although his hearing was as acute as that of a wolf, he was just beyond the reach of his gift. He could hear only the echoes of voices too many and too distant to make out their words.

He jumped down and looked to the right. The rushing sound of water indicated the river that ran behind the property. He led the horse five minutes southeast and arrived at a spot he had not visited since that last fateful night, the last time he saw Mihaela. He turned the animal loose to quench its thirst and walked around the circular area. It looked both the same and different. Eight hundred years had passed, changing the landscape here and there—the river eroding away some areas, and plant growth overshadowing other spots. But in all, it looked the same. He would bring her here, he thought, before taking her to his home. Mark smiled and settled down upon the thick grass to wait. When the moonrise begins its descent, when all the others were asleep, he would go to his woman and claim her once and for all, and woe be to anyone who gets in his way.

He lay staring up at the night sky. That last night, he'd left this glen with a promise to her that they would be together. When he returned, she was nowhere to be found. He'd gone after Petrescu thinking the man was responsible, and the bastard claimed no knowledge. His own people believed him and the search for Mihaela began. Marku had returned home to face his father only to be shut down and ordered to forget the gypsy girl and marry Alexandra. His own guilt and shame had answered for him when he agreed to honor his family's obligation and go through with the wedding, but his heart would not permit him to do it. He'd left in the middle of the night to join the search. Each minute that passed meant his Mihaela was in danger, and the longer they waited to find her, the less likely she would survive.

He'd set out heading for the gypsy camp, fear and anxiety gripping his heart. He never made it. Not far from his destination, he'd flown off his horse and lost consciousness. He still didn't know exactly what happened, but when he woke the next night, he was filled with a thirst so demanding, he couldn't ignore it, and what he thirsted for was not water or wine, but blood. His first victim had been his horse. The attack was so savage, the animal was mutilated. But that had not satisfied his bloodlust. He was not far from the Curarya camp, and blind need led him to the site where he massacred nearly the entire tribe including Mihaela's father, Simion. When his thirst had been slaked, he focused on their faces searching for Petrescu. Of all of them, it was his blood he wanted most. Even in his frenzy, his heartbreak was still far more painful.

"Where is he?" he demanded. The fools ran from him, but he was faster. He leapt upon them, draining them dry. He found Petrescu's parents, and they refused to tell him what he wanted to know.

"Where is your son? Where is that coward? What has he done to Mihaela?" Marku watched as they made the sign of the cross backing up.

Janus Petrescu shielded his wife. "He is not here, demon! Be gone!"

Marku laughed, his eyes glowing amber. "Then you will do." He grabbed the older Petrescu sinking his elongated fangs deep into the old man's neck. Blood spurted from the vein like a fountain offering life-giving drink. He could hear Janus's wife screaming behind them, and it only added to the ecstasy. When he tossed the old man's body away from him, he turned and smiled down upon the mother of his enemy. "Are you ready to tell me what I want to know?" He stepped closer.

She scrambled backwards, terror in her eyes. "He is not here. My husband did not lie!"

"Then where is your wayward son, madam?" Marku cornered her, leaning down and placing his hands on the ground at either side of her head. "Tell me and I will spare your life."

Tears ran down her cheeks. She glanced at her husband, clearly thinking quickly. "I don't know where he is now. He was with Magdalena yesterday. That's all I know. Please!"

Marku cocked his head sideways like the predator he now was, staring into her eyes. "And who is Magdalena?"

"She's the village elder. Our shaman."

"Where will I find her?"

"On the edge of the village, north. She lives apart from us as is her wish." The woman shrank back.

He placed a hand on her cheek, caressing softly, and smiled. "There, now. See how easy that was?"

She held still, not daring to breathe. "Not easy at all. You've already taken my life." Her tortured eyes went to rest on the body of her dead husband.

"Already?" He looked over his shoulder at Janus. "Well, then, I suppose I should just finish the job."

She caught his meaning a half-second too late as Marku gripped her head, twisting it sharply to the left until her neck snapped. She slumped down, dead.

He left then, heading for the north side of the village. As soon as he found this Magdalena, he would get the information he needed, kill Petrescu, and locate Mihaela. He just knew the filthy gypsy dog had something to do with her disappearance. And if he discovered that the man had killed his love, he was going to make Petrescu suffer pain like he'd never imagined.

Dracula snorted, snuffling the grass at the side of the river. The sound pulled Mark back to the present. He remembered his darkest moments as vividly as if they had just happened. He'd never found Petrescu or Mihaela, but he had found Magdalena, and to his astonishment, had been unable to lay hands on her. The gypsy witch possessed powerful magic, had damn near killed him, and he'd had to run away, seeking shelter from the rising sun. His life had never been the same since.

Over the decades, he'd managed to control his bloodlust, matured, one could say, and even mellowed out. He was even appalled by his actions then although not in the least sorry about wanting to kill the man he knew in his heart was responsible for the disappearance of Mihaela. Still, with the reappearance of her in his life, reincarnated as Meghan, he was once again moved by the love in his heart, and not the bloodlust inherent in his vampirism. He chuckled. When he realized then what he'd become, he was able to fill in some of the blank spaces in his memory. He must've been attacked by a vampire on his way to the gypsy camp that night. It was the only explanation. But what he didn't understand fully was how Petrescu had survived all these hundreds of years. Magdalena seemed to be the only possible reason. His own mother said he'd visited the shaman the day before, the same night Mark's life had changed. The bastard must've been making a deal with the old devil herself to steal Mihaela's life and ensure his own. For that alone, he still wanted to kill him. And he was thrilled that he would actually get the chance.

Mark had long ago given up ever getting his revenge, but Petrescu's longevity, however he achieved it, was both good news for Mark, and bad news for Peter. But first, he would get his woman.

He glanced at the moon, noticing its position in the night sky. His ears told him that the revelry down by the campfire had died down. He stood up and peered in that direction. His keen sight didn't reveal anyone walking about. Further down from the glen where he stood was a row of cabins, five in all, and each was filled with occupants. He wasn't worried about them. He looked for his horse who stood resting quietly.

"Stay here and behave. I'll be back soon...with our woman," he told the beast.

Mark set out, heading for the main house. His senses, psychically connected to Meghan, led him without fault. When he reached the house, he could see everyone had gone to bed. The fire in the pit was nearly extinguished leaving the scent of burnt wood on the air. He approached the solid double doors. Reaching out, he turned the knob slowly. It wasn't locked, but when he tried stepping over the threshold, an invisible barrier blocked him. He'd not been invited in, so could not enter.

He closed the door and walked around the perimeter letting his connection to Meghan guide him. When he came around the back of the house, he looked up. There was a balcony on the second floor. He scaled the wall and perched on the concrete ledge. French-style doors stood open, letting the breeze inside. He could hear her breathing softly, slowly. She was asleep. Another sound joined hers, another deep breathing. He sniffed the air like a wolf. Curarya. It was the little gypsy. Meghan was not alone, and he could not physically go inside, but he didn't need to. He sent his thoughts outward and found entry to her dreams through the psychic marks he'd already left imprinted.

Meghan sighed. Someone was nuzzling her neck, dropping soft kisses on her tender skin. The tingles running down her spine lit her body on fire with need. She turned her face seeking the lips caressing her. They found hers immediately and claimed her, devouring her mouth, and leaving her breathless. Finally, they pulled away.

"Have you missed me, Mihaela?"

Meghan had grown used to hearing him refer to her by this name. It felt right somehow. "Yes. But I don't understand," she said.

"What is it you don't understand?" His hand cupped her chin as his thumb softly stroked her cheek.

"The others. They say you want to hurt me. Is it true?" She tried to look up at him, but as always, the shadows hid his face. Still, the veil had been lifted in her subconscious earlier when Dana revealed his identity to her. She knew who it was.

"Who says this?" he demanded.

"The old woman. All of them, the gypsies. They say you're a monster who wants to kill me."

The hurt in her voice pained his heart. He held her face gently with both hands. "Mihaela, I would never hurt you. I've only just found you again, and there is no way I will allow anyone between us. I love you. I've always loved you. Do you believe me?" He searched her eyes.

She paused, sorting through her feelings. "Yes. Yes, I believe you."

"And do you love me?" His deep voice held a note of desperation.

"I do." Her reply sounded sweet to his ears and touched his desiccated heart.

"Then come with me. Come be with me, now. There is a place I want to show you."

Meghan heard the excitement in his voice and it was infectious. "What is this place?"

"You've seen it many times. I take you there in your dreams, but I want you to see it with your eyes, not just through my memories. Come. Rise up out of your bed and step out onto the balcony." He stepped back, retreating.

She felt his loss immediately. "Wait! Don't go." She reached for him, but found nothing.

"I'm right outside." His voice rumbled deep, soothing her.

Meghan sat up and placed her feet on the floor. Still caught up inside the dream, she stood and followed the direction that the sound of his words indicated. Each step brought her closer, and as she drew near, the dream began to fade as her mind awakened. She stopped, looking around and wondering how she got where she was.

"I am here, Mihaela."

The familiar voice beckoned and her heart raced. She tiptoed to the door, peering through the opening. Her eyes located the tall, dark figure. The man stood leaning casually with his arms crossed over his chest. He wore all black from head to toe, and he was the sexiest man she'd ever seen. He was solid, muscular, and real. Meghan opened the door and stepped one foot out onto the balcony. He lifted his head and smiled.

"It's really you." She whispered her words, awe and fear mixed within them.

He heard it. "Don't be afraid. I will not hurt you. I would rather die than hurt you." He searched her face.

Meghan could see the sincerity in his expression. His dark eyes, framed by long lashes, held hers. He was every bit as handsome as she remembered from the tavern, and her body responded to his presence, desiring his arms around her. The carnal memory of her dreams from the past week caused her to blush as she recalled everything they'd done together, every place his hands had touched, every inch of skin his lips had tasted, and the complete possession he took when he entered her willing body, thrusting deep, and wringing unbelievable ecstasy from her soul. The slow, sexy grin that began to spread across his full lips told her he knew where her thoughts wandered.

The smile disappeared when he caught sight of the locket hanging around her slender neck. He stared at the thing nestled between her breasts just below the neckline of her thin gown. "Do you still love me, Mihaela?" He sought her eyes again, asking the question once more now that she was awake.

Meghan hesitated, torn between the wild feelings lighting her body on fire, and the warning still ringing in her ears from Adina. "I don't know what to say. Why is everyone warning me about you? Why do they think you want to hurt me? We've met only once. I don't understand."

"Because they don't understand. They don't know who I am. They don't know who you are."

"Who am I?" She was confused.

"You are Mihaela. You are the only woman I've ever loved, and I can't believe you're here. I can't believe fate would give me a second chance after it snatched you away from me. I don't deserve it."

The anguish in his words ripped at her heart. She reached for his hand, but he pulled away as if she'd burned him. She stopped.

"That makes no sense to me." She waited, and then asked, "Who are you?"

"It would be easier to show you. The story is long and complicated." He sighed, dropping his hands to his sides.

"Then show me," she demanded.

He looked at the necklace. Her eyes followed.

"What? This?" She pulled it out from her gown and he backed up. "You mean this actually works?" She saw the truth in his retreat. She lifted an eyebrow.

"I can show you, but you will have to remove that." He pointed at the jewelry.

"Adina said I was never to remove this. Why?" Meghan looked up at him.

"Because it hurts me. It can kill me, because of what I am." The sadness in his tone touched her.

"A vampire." Meghan said the word out loud, feeling completely silly.

"Yes," he confirmed.

"You're really a vampire?" The incredulity in her voice rose.

"Sssh," he whispered. "Yes, I am a vampire, and no, I am not going to kill you. I can show you everything with a touch," he held out his hand, "but only if you remove the talisman. Otherwise, you, and only you will be the death of me, and after eight-hundred years, that is saying something."

"Eight-hundred?" The shock in her eyes caused him to chuckle.

"Yes. I guess you could say I'm the proverbial older man to you. But at one time, we were the same age."

Meghan blew out a breath. This was getting weirder than it already was. She fingered the locket while she considered her options. He leaned back against the wall, his hand still out, palm up, waiting.

"What's your name?"

He stood straighter. "Marku Andrei Anghelescu or, just *Mark* at your service." He proffered a courtly bow.

The name sank in, and something inside Meghan unlocked by one tumbler. There were more tumblers to go, but she needed answers to get them to fall into place. She made her decision, and reaching up, she unclasped the chain and set the necklace on the balcony ledge. Without further hesitation, she placed her hand in his and stepped inside the circle of his arms.

It was electric. The simple touch of his skin against hers felt like a current running throughout her entire body. Meghan looked at their clasped hands in wonder, but when she looked at Mark's face, she was stunned. He was staring at her in complete awe. There was both happiness and pain in his dark eyes, and the smile that trembled on his lips slowly spread into a full-fledged expression of pure joy.

His fingers entangled in her own even as his free hand came up to caress her cheek gently. "Finally, after so long, you are here."

His deep whisper sent shivers down Meghan's spine. Her skin instantly puckered with gooseflesh and when his thumb skimmed her lower lip, tingles danced over her body. "How is this possible?" she asked.

"Because you are mine," he growled, "And I am yours!" And then his lips found hers. The kiss exploded as his tongue sought the innermost warmth of her mouth sweeping, delving deep, and drowning Meghan in desire. His arms reached around and pulled her close. His hands roamed her back, gripping and caressing, kneading and molding her softness into his hardness.

Heat spread out from her core like a wildfire. As close as she already was, her body wanted to be closer. Mark nibbled her lips and then soothed them with soft kisses. His large, strong hands slid down to cup her rounded derriere, his fingers gently squeezing as he lifted her up onto her toes until her center rested against his growing desire. She moaned into his mouth as he thrust his hips forward while he gripped her pliable flesh. The rubbing motion had Meghan wrapping one leg around his waist. His hand slid to her knee lifting it higher creating the opening he needed to hit her sweet spot.

His lips left hers to trail down her neck, nipping here and there. Meghan wanted more. She needed to remove the barriers between them.

"Mark, please," she whimpered.

He smiled into her fragrant hair. "Please what, Mihaela?"

"Please!" she panted.

He knew she was close. He knew her body then, and he knew it now after a week of erotic dreams. He stopped. "Not here."

"What? No!" Meghan stared at him, shocked.

Mark tried to keep the smile from his face. "Not with your friend inside. Come with me." He stepped back.

"Where?" Meghan felt frustrated. Her body was filled with heat, her blood thick and pulsing between her legs.

"Trust me. We'll be there in no time at all, and then we will have all the time in the world for this." He pulled her against him again, his erection pressed against her through both of their clothing. Mark could see her lower lip protruding in an unconscious pout. "It's as painful for me as well, my love, I promise, but it will be worth it. We'll finally be together."

He leaned his forehead against hers, and Meghan's resolve melted away. She trusted him. In their short and strange time together, he'd only ever brought her pleasure, had only ever been kind, sweet, and tender.

"Okay. I'll go grab my clothes and shoes and meet you out front." She dropped a quick kiss on his lips and ran inside on tiptoes.

Mark waited until she was out of sight, and then in one quick motion, leapt over the side and landed two stories below. He ran around to the front and when she appeared coming out the main door, he took her hand and led her off to the woods. Behind them, the occupants of the house slept on.

Chapter 9

"This is it." After walking for nearly twenty minutes, they arrived in a clearing. Mark spread his arms wide and spun around to face her.

Meghan stood in the middle of the clearing, looking around. She had a strong feeling of déjà vu.

"I've been here before," she said, her expression reflecting her inner turmoil.

She walked to a grassy spot and sat down, feeling the ground with her hands. Then she glanced up at the night sky, listening.

"There's a stream around here, a small river." She glanced over her shoulder and pointed. "Back there." She turned quickly to look at him. "How do I know that? How could I have ever been here before?"

Mark joined her on the grass, sitting on his knees and facing her.

"You have been here before," he said. He reached out to take her hands in his. "It was simply in another lifetime. It was when you were mine. My Mihaela." He waited for her to absorb that information.

"That was my name then?" Her eyes sought his.

"Yes."

"And we were a couple?"

He caressed her palms with his fingers. "Yes. We were going to get married."

"You said you would show me. Show me now." She inched closer, her knees opening to keep him in front of her.

"Lean forward." He let go of her hands and placed his on either side of her head. "Close your eyes."

Meghan did as bid. Nothing seemed to be happening. She opened them again. "Well?"

It was daylight, and everything around her looked different.

"Mark, where are you?" Meghan stood up and spun around. She nearly tripped on her skirt.

Skirt? Looking down, she saw the long length of red and gold material that swirled around her ankles and rested on the top of her worn leather boots. Above her waist, the red material was cinched with a black and gold threaded corset that was tied so tight, her breasts nearly spilled out over the top.

"What in the world?" She looked up in time to notice she was standing in the middle of a small village. There were people gathered around, watching her. Meghan glanced left and saw a well, and then she looked to her right and straight into the eyes of the one man who made her skin crawl.

"Mihaela, you have no choice in this matter. You will do as your father says and we will be married tomorrow. Then you will be mine!" The tall man sneered at his cornered bride to be.

"Professor Petrescu?" Meghan backed away from the look of intense anger on his face. Rage rolled off him in waves striking fear in her heart. Desperate, she took two more steps back as he slowly approached.

Feeling behind her, Meghan found the ledge of the well. "Don't come any closer! I will jump down this well if you do!" Grasping the edge, she sat upon it, swinging one leg over. *Why did I just say that?*

"If you attempt to jump, I will make sure you wish you were successful!" said Peter. He was within arms-length of her now. Meghan spit in his face.

"You will be sorry for that!" And with lightning speed, Peter swung out with his right hand. The hit landed making her cheek explode with pain even as she was brutally dragged by her hair off the well and thrown to the ground.

She sucked in a breath, hiding her face and fearing another blow. When it didn't come, she peeked up through her fingers. The scene shifted and Mark was standing before her, only now, he was dressed in a white, flowing shirt, vest, and dark suede trousers covered to the knee by black leather riding boots. His hair was a bit longer and tied back with a cord. He held out his hand.

"This is how we first met. This is where I first saw you." Although his manner of dress had changed, it was the Mark from her time speaking.

Meghan allowed him to help her up.

"I don't understand. That man was Professor Petrescu." She pointed back at the well where all the people had been standing around. No one was there any longer. Day had once again turned to night, and she was again dressed in her jeans, sweater, and boots.

She was back in the glen, sitting in front of him. Confusion marred her features.

"Yes and no. That was Peter Petrescu, a gypsy dog who once tried to claim you."

"But that's the same name." Meghan was having a difficult time understanding. She shook her head trying to clear it and think rationally, but none of this was rational. "Is he like me? A reincarnation of sorts? Is that why he showed an interest?"

Mark fought against his response to her words. Inside, he wanted to kill the man, but until Meghan fully comprehended the situation, he needed to remain in control. "No, he is not like you. He's filth." He cupped her face, leaning in and staring into her eyes intensely. "He is not an ancestor of Peter Petrescu, he is the original."

He let the words sink in and watched as disbelief clouded her brown eyes. "That's not possible." She shook her head and leaned back.

"I might normally agree with you. Perhaps if he was like me, a vampire, but he's not. And yet, it is true, nonetheless. I can smell it on him. The same scent, the same blood. A vampire's nose is never wrong."

"But that's crazy! How can he be alive hundreds of years later? And you said he tried once to claim me. What does that mean anyway?" Meghan pulled her knees beneath her and sat up straight. She wanted answers.

Mark blew out a breath. "He was your fiancé."

"What! There is no way I would agree to marry that man. He's creepy!" She hugged herself.

Mark chuckled, but it was a dark sound. "You didn't agree. Mihaela's father, Simion, made the arrangement with Janus Petrescu in order to raise himself up in the hierarchy of the tribe."

"Tribe?" A furrow appeared between Meghan's delicate brows.

"I may have forgotten to mention it, but you were a gypsy also." He offered a half-smile. "Lovarya. Actually, a cousin to your friend, the little Curarya gypsy."

This surprised Meghan, but at the same time, felt right. She loosened her arms, letting her hands slide to rest on her thighs. "Well, that explains a lot," she said, looking around.

"Explains what?" he asked, curious.

She looked at him. "Why I felt drawn to Romania, why it felt like I'd come home the moment I stepped off the airplane." She smiled, but it faded quickly. "So, my own father sold me out?

Or Mihaela's. This is really confusing. How did I...she... get out of it? Please tell me that then me didn't marry that creep!"

He shook his head. "No, you didn't. After that day, after I looked into your eyes, I knew you were the one. Seeing that filthy peasant mistreat you, well, needless to say, I wasn't having it. My father owned this land then. I own it now. I went to Simion and offered him a deal he could not refuse. I gave him riches, he gave me you."

Meghan laughed. It sounded so outdated, so ridiculously old-fashioned that she couldn't take it seriously. "You know no one does that sort of thing anymore, right?"

Seeing her laugh, even if it was at him, calmed him and Mark enjoyed seeing her light of heart and not afraid of him. "Is that so, Miss Hartley?"

"You're darn right it's so. So, what happened? I imagine Petrescu was not happy." She waited to hear the rest of the story.

"No, he certainly was not, but there wasn't anything he could do about it. Oh, he tried. We had an altercation or two where I got to pound his face a few times." He glanced at her, grinning. "I really did like that part, but it did him no good. You were mine." The grin faded and an intense possessiveness returned to his eyes.

Meghan felt those last three words vibrate down her spine and spread like warm honey throughout her body. "And I agreed to this?" She licked her suddenly dry lips.

Mark, sensing the change in her body, leaned forward, and inched closer on his hands and knees, stalking her like the predator he was. "Oh, yes. You insisted on it." His face leaned in close to her own. She felt the sensuality rippling over him, reaching out to her.

"I insisted?"

"Well, you wanted me, very badly..."

His lips hovered over her own. Meghan felt hot despite the cold night. Still, she shivered.

"Are you cold?" he asked, concerned.

Mark didn't feel the cold, or the heat for that matter. He almost forgot she was human and subject to the elements. He rubbed her arms with his large hands trying to instill heat with friction through her thick sweater.

"I'm okay," she said, glancing down at his hands, and then up into his face. "Were you a vampire then?"

Mark smiled slowly, continuing the rubbing motion, then moving his hands to her back, sliding down, and lifting her beneath her buttocks until he settled her onto his lap. He wanted to place himself between her body and the cold ground thinking he was at least a little less cold than the frosty grass.

"I was as human then as you are now. My... condition didn't happen until later. As a matter of fact, it happened on the night we were running off to get married."

Meghan was feeling warmer. His ministrations had set off a spark of heat that was being slowly kindled to a flame by his dexterous fingers.

"How did it happen? Was I there?" She let him hold her closer. He tucked her head under his chin and kissed her hair.

"No. You weren't with me when it happened. I still don't exactly know how it happened. You see, you'd disappeared—"

"Disappeared?" She cut in. "How?"

"I don't know, my love. I came back here to meet up with you in our glen. You never showed up, and when I set out to find you, something happened, and I blacked out. I awoke the next night, frantic." He left out the details about his insane bloodlust. "I went to Simion thinking he'd reneged somehow, that maybe Petrescu had taken you, but he knew nothing, and I never did find that rat bastard. The last I knew came from his own parents who claimed he'd gone to the village shaman, an old gypsy witch who was their village elder. I could get nothing from her, and in fact, barely escaped with my life."

"From an old woman?" Meghan tilted her head up to look at him.

Mark smoothed her hair, winding the blonde tresses around and around his fingers, letting the silkiness slip through. "She was a powerful witch, a sorceress of great power."

"Why would Petrescu go to her?"

"I can only imagine, but I'd say his longevity has something to do with it. But why? Why would he seek to stay alive so long? That is what I don't get. And I never did find out what happened to you. I'm just thankful to have you back." He kissed the tip of her nose.

"But, Mark, I'm not her anymore. Even though some of this feels familiar, I'm still Meghan, not Mihaela."

He nodded. "This is true. A part of her is in there, and you are who you are now. But Meghan, the soul you carry," he touched a finger to her chest, over her heart, "is the soul that I love, and I don't mind at all getting to know you all over again."

He didn't want to tell her that despite her new persona in this life, she still looked like, acted like, and felt in his arms, just like Mihaela. Some things do not change when souls are reborn. He would accept her new identity. He didn't care, as long as she was by his side.

Meghan studied his face. She was thinking about everything he'd shown her, and every word he'd said. It felt like an episode of the Twilight Zone, but at the same time, she knew it was all true. Stranger than her acceptance of the story were her feelings for this man. He'd lived a long time with no hope whatsoever of finding the woman he loved, this Mihaela, or her. Whatever! Her mind was mixed up. And yet, here she was, cradled in his lap, held securely in his arms, smack in the middle of a glen she weirdly remembered. They weren't two strangers now. She wasn't the reincarnated version of an ancient gypsy girl, and he wasn't a mythical, blood-sucking monster of legend. They were just a man and a woman gazing at each other under the stars.

Her heart melted. This felt right to her, and it didn't matter that Dana's grandmother had warned her about the vicious Strigoi. Mark wasn't vicious. He was kind, sweet, and sexy. The last part hadn't completely escaped her. Wasn't it only an hour or so ago they were making out on the balcony?

His lips stretched into a smile. "I did promise you we'd finish that."

Before Meghan could utter her surprise at his reading her thoughts, his mouth found hers, taking her lips in a breathtaking kiss. The flame he'd sparked earlier with his wandering hands erupted into an inferno. She threw caution to the wind and kissed him back. It was even better than her dreams.

"I know," he whispered into her mouth.

His hands roamed freely, caressing her back before sliding lower and squeezing her buttocks. He nibbled a path to her ear, licked, and then continued down her neck where the heat of her skin combined with the scent of her blood. The heady aphrodisiac hardened his manhood and lengthened his fangs. He longed to sink both deep inside her and claim her under the starry sky. His fingers found her breast, rubbing the tip, and making her nipple pucker, begging for more.

"Mark, please!" Meghan moaned her demand.

"With pleasure, my love." He parted the sweater revealing the flannel plaid beneath. *Thank goodness, it's a button-down,* he thought. One by one, the buttons were undone until her naked breasts greeted his hungry gaze. "Frumoasa," he uttered, before his lips descended, taking the hardened peak into his mouth. He licked her nipple with his tongue, then suckled it until she gripped his hair, desperate for satisfaction.

Barely able to think, Meghan grasped onto the word he'd whispered. "What does that mean?"

Reluctant to release his prize, Mark gently bit the peak, then applying one last lick, lifted his head and buried his seeking lips into her neck, whispering, "Beautiful. It means beautiful."

Meghan smiled as she loosened her grip on his hair. She allowed her fingers to comb through his dark strands. They felt every bit as soft as she first imagined when she noticed him in the tavern.

"I'm glad my hair pleases you." He nipped her earlobe.

"Stop that!" she giggled.

"What? This?" He nipped it again, then soothed the spot with gentle kisses.

"No, reading my mind. How do you do that?"

Mark lifted his head and found her lips again, searing them with the heat of his passion. When she whimpered her need, he pulled back.

"We are connected, my love. It is a psychic bond formed when I visited your dreams."

Meghan stopped. She looked up at him. "That was an invasion of my privacy, you know. I didn't invite you to... to..." She struggled to find the right words.

"To enter your personal space?" Mark added helpfully.

"Yes. That!" Meghan gave him a very serious look.

He knew she was right, but somehow, he wasn't as sorry as he should be. "You're right. Do you wish it hadn't happened?" He held her close to his body, slowly laying her back and shifting his weight over her, sliding a knee between hers even as he pressed her into the soft, but cold grass.

"Well…" She thought about it. *Am I really sorry? He never hurt me. Wait, yes he did. He bit me!*

Mark chuckled. "I did, and I'm sorry. I promise never to do that again unless you invite me to. But we did a lot of other things that you didn't mind, like this…" He settled his hips against hers, the evidence of his desire pushed into the most intimate part of her, rubbing slowly and insistently up and down. The friction of his jeans on hers only caused more heat as liquid warmth spread out from her center.

"Well, that wasn't a bad thing," she agreed. Her breath caught as she wrapped her knees around him as he thrust again.

"And this." Mark suddenly rolled over, carrying Meghan with him. His strong hands lifted her up until she straddled him. He gripped her hips and rolled her over the stiff length of him. When she moaned uncontrollably, he grinned. "You are killing me. My God, you are so breathtaking."

He gazed up at the woman riding him. Her head was thrown back in abandon, her hair spilling down her back. Her shirt and sweater were still parted revealing her magnificent breasts in the moonlight. The extension of her neck beckoned him even as his fevered eyes narrowed on the pulse in her jugular. With each beat of her heart, it throbbed, and each time it did, he thrust his hips while gliding hers forward and back along his length. He couldn't believe they were dry-humping like teenagers when he craved to bury himself inside of her warmth, but the moment was beyond erotic, and he was enjoying watching her take her pleasure.

He reached up with one hand and cupped her breast, rolling the nipple between his thumb and forefinger. She continued riding him as he massaged and pinched the soft flesh. The pleasure/pain had her panting.

"Oh, God, Mark. Please."

"I'm yours, Mihaela. Take me where you wish. Ride me!" The friction was driving him wild. Her womanly scent rose upon the heat created by their bodies rubbing together. He was sure he would burst into flames at any moment. She leaned forward planting her hands on his chest. His own hand abandoned her softness to dig into her hips. He thrust and rubbed while she countered. Each movement caused her gorgeous breast to sway above him. Meghan was lost in ecstasy, and Mark was right there with her. Without further thought, he unbuttoned her jeans, tugged the zipper down and when she leaned forward again, slid his hand inside. His dexterous fingers found her moist crevice and entered the wet folds. When he pressed her nub, Meghan exploded, climaxing hard.

"Oh, my God! Yes!" She pushed harder as his fingertips massaged her heated flesh. Her body shuddered and her muscles twitched low in her stomach.

Before she could come down from the high, Mark flipped her over, tugged her jeans off right over her boots. He shoved them beneath her bottom with one hand and undid his own jeans with the other.

Meghan watched in amazement as his rod sprang forth. It wasn't the first one she'd ever seen, but it was by far the largest, and before she could say a word, Mark positioned himself between her thighs and plunged deep. She sucked in a breath. The immense pleasure of him inside her was more than she could stand, and when he cradled her head in his hands and kissed her, she forgot what she was going to say. His tongue tangled with her own as he thoroughly claimed her mouth.

"Mine!" he said, and then pulled out almost to his tip before thrusting hard. He repeated the motion and her hips rose to meet him. Mark reached down with one hand to grasp her beneath her knee. He hitched her leg high over his waist opening her wider allowing him to delve deeper.

Meghan gripped his shoulders and held on for dear life as each hard thrust propelled her toward another orgasm. She couldn't even catch her breath. He claimed her just as surely as he had in her dreams, only this was better. A hundred times better!

"Say it! Say you're mine," he demanded. His lips hovered over hers. He ground his hips down on hers again.

She looked into his eyes. The dark depths were glowing amber, and she saw the white of a long fang peeking out from his mouth. She should've been terrified, but he'd proven already he wouldn't harm her, and he'd promised not to bite her unless she invited him.

"I'm yours." Saying it was easier than she expected. Meghan bit her lip. "Would it hurt?"

Mark blinked, confused. "Would what hurt? Am I hurting you, love?" He stopped thrusting, but it nearly killed him.

Meghan pushed her hips high encouraging him to continue. "No, you're not hurting me. I want to know, if you bite me, will it hurt?"

He smiled slowly. "Initially, yes, like a pinprick, but my bite will also give you pleasure beyond your wildest dreams. And Meghan," he caressed her scalp with his fingers, "it will bond us further. I'll always know your thoughts, know where you are. If you let me do it more than once, the bond will only grow stronger. I will crave only you, only your blood. No one else's."

The pleasure she was feeling right then was already intense. She couldn't imagine it getting any better, but he said it could, that it would, if she allowed it. And he'd called her Meghan, not Mihaela. He wasn't making love to a ghost anymore, but to her. Her heart flooded with feelings.

"Bite me," she whispered.

His eyes popped wide. "Are you sure?"

"I am. Bite me, Mark. Make me yours."

He looked at her in awe. "You are the bravest, most beautiful, and trusting woman. I don't deserve you." Mark's eyes moistened. "But I will cherish you like no other, and your happiness will be my life's mission. You will be mine, Meghan," he kissed her lips softly, then lifted his head to stare into her eyes, "and I will be eternally yours."

Loved filled her, body and soul, and then the pleasure rolled her as his hips picked up the rhythm, increasing it, and taking them higher. Just as she came to the very precipice of climax, he sank his fangs into the soft flesh of her neck while sinking his rod deep to the hilt. The world exploded in color!

The cold was replaced by warmth, as if the sun had come out. She no longer felt the frost under her back, but she did feel the overpowering orgasm that swept over her entire body. She shuddered as wave upon wave crashed over her. Her fingers clutched his head to her, and he drank. With each sip of her life-giving nectar, their bond strengthened. Meghan felt not only her pleasure, but his as well, and it was mind-blowing.

What seemed to last forever ended all too soon in her opinion. Mark released her neck, licking the site where his teeth punctured her skin. His saliva healed the spot in seconds.

Languor settled into their limbs, and they lay wrapped in each other's arms.

"That was..." She started to speak.

"Freaking incredible!" He chuckled, and the deep rumble of his voice vibrated against her chest.

Mark rolled off her and eased up onto his elbow. A smile remained fixed on his face as he slowly buttoned up her shirt and pulled her sweater around her. "As much as it pains me to say it, you need to put your pants back on before you freeze." He got up to help her.

Meghan took his hand, standing up. He handed her the jeans she'd been wearing. She struggled to get them up over the boots she still had on. The absurdity of it made her laugh. Mark readjusted, and zipped and buttoned his own jeans. A soft snort interrupted them.

"What was that?" Meghan pulled her shirt and sweater down over her pants and wrapped her arms around her body.

Mark clucked his tongue, and a large, black stallion came trotting toward him from the direction of the river. "It's only my horse." The beast stopped in front of him and tossed his head. Mark reached back to Meghan. "Come, meet Dracula."

"Dracula?" she replied, her brows quirked with humor. "You're a vampire and you named your horse Dracula?" She stepped closer allowing him to take her hand in his and place it on the horse's soft muzzle.

He grinned. "I know. It amused me at the time."

"He's gorgeous. Hello, Dracula, I'm Meghan." She spoke low as she stroked his nose.

The stallion sniffed her hand, and then nuzzled deeper into her palm seeking more rubs.

"He's obviously a highly discriminating animal. He knows a beautiful woman when he sees her." Mark stood behind her wrapping his arms around her waist.

"Is this how you got here? You must live close by."

"I do. Would you like to see my place?" He dropped a kiss into her hair. "I would love to show you." He waited, hoping she would choose on her own to come with him. He didn't know what he would do if she decided against it.

Meghan considered her options. She could go with him, see his home, throwing caution to the wind. *Haven't I done that already?* Or she could call it a night and go back to the Veleru's, climb into her warm bed, and think about him, all alone, and feeling guilty as sin for ignoring the warning her new gypsy family had issued. They meant well, of course. She knew that. Mark's arms slipped from around her waist and Meghan feared she'd waited too long to answer. He might be feeling rejected. A soft thud sounded, and she turned.

"Mark, I'm not sure—"

He was lying in the grass, unmoving. Behind him, a dark figure stood in the shadow of the moon. It raised its hand and blew. Dust flew in her face, the world spun, and Meghan felt her knees give out as she fell forward. She was unconscious before she hit the ground.

Chapter 10

Dana rolled over and tried to snuggle down into the covers. She shivered, a chill invading her cocoon. She cracked an eye and looked around. The door. It was still open. She'd forgotten that earlier she and Meghan had cracked open the French doors to let fresh air in to alleviate the stuffiness in her old room. She would have to get up to shut it, but that meant climbing out from under her covers. She sighed, sat up, and opened both eyes. The bed across from her was empty.

"Meghan?" Dana stood, looking around the room. She walked to the open door and peeked out. No one was on the balcony, so she closed and locked it. The cold air slid over her skin, and an urgent need hit her bladder. Dana ran down the hall to the bathroom. She expected to find Meghan either there or on her way back to their room, but an empty restroom greeted her. Taking a moment, she took care of business, and then went downstairs to find her friend. After a search of the living room and kitchen, and even a quick peek out the front door, she knew it had happened. He'd taken her.

"Grandmother!" she shouted as she ran back up the stairs. The commotion woke her younger brother, Sorin, who poked his head out of his bedroom.

"What is with the shouting, Dana?" He stood shirtless in pajama pants, appearing rumpled and annoyed to be awakened.

"The Strigoi! He took Meghan!" Tears clogged her throat as panic swallowed her up.

Adina Veleru walked out of her room at the end of the hall. She stood calmly, taking in the scene. "So, he has breached our defenses." She turned her wizened eyes upon Sorin. "Go wake Cosmin and Stefan. Tell them to get the women and children here immediately. You and your cousins take the rifles and the wooden bullets, go get your father and the rest. We must all circle the wagons, and then, we go find her." She pulled her shawl around her frail shoulders and shuffled to the stairwell. "Dana, bring my box from my bedroom, the one beneath my bed." She began a slow descent down the steps as her granddaughter ran to her room to retrieve the box, and Sorin ducked inside his own room to get dressed.

In ten minutes, they met up in the living room. Sorin slipped on his coat and picked up three rifles, slinging two over his shoulder by their straps, and grabbed a couple of boxes of wooden bullets. They were handmade by the Curarya. Inside the center of each was a sliver of iron. The wood was an amalgam of sawdust and silver. The silver and iron weakened vampires while the wood lodged in their already desiccated hearts killed them. He left to awaken his brother, father, and cousin.

Dana stood, holding the old wooden box. Where once it was probably a dark brown wood, it was now black with age. The panels showed wear from ancestral hands, and it was bound by an iron lock.

"How will we find her, grandmama? If he has her, she may already be...," she swallowed past the painful lump in her throat as she struggled to say the word, "...dead."

"Tish, child. Bring me the box." Adina sat in the easy chair and waited as Dana placed the miniature chest on the coffee table. She pulled a length of leather, hanging around her thin neck, out from beneath her nightgown. A metal key hung from it looking like a remnant from another time. She lifted it over her head and slid the key into the lock. It creaked and groaned, and then clicked.

Dana sat down on the end of the couch closest to her grand-mother and peered inside the box. Resting on a bed of faded red velvet were several items that she'd never seen before.

"What are they?"

Adina lifted out the first item, a long silver chain with an unusual pendant. The pendant was a large piece of dark, smoky quartz. As she held it up to the light of the lamp, Dana saw that it had a reddish center. Adina set it down on the table. She pulled forth the next item which was a smaller wooden box. It appeared Asian in origin. The wood was teak, and the top slid sideways exposing small vials within, thirteen in all. The box took its place next to the pendant. A small bronze bowl joined the other items, and finally, the old woman lifted out a parchment that was folded over. The paper was yellowed with time, and delicate.

"These are your inheritance. They pass down through only the women in our family." Adina looked at her granddaughter.

"Then why are they not with mama?" Dana asked the logical question.

The older woman reached out and took Dana's hand. She flipped it over and traced the line in her palm that ran from the space between her thumb and index finger to the lower, outside edge just above her wrist. "The box passes to the next clan shaman. The gift sometimes skips a generation. Your mother does not have the mark, but you do." She pointed to a small crisscross over her lifeline. It was star-shaped, and something Dana had not noticed before. In fact, she was sure it had never been there before.

"I see your confusion, and you are right. It is something new. The mark shows when the power is triggered. Yours was most likely triggered the first night you encountered the Strigoi."

Dana blinked. "But what if I don't want to be a shaman? I have a career, grandmama."

"You don't choose the power, Dana. The power chooses you, and it only chooses those who are worthy. It is not something you can refuse. It simply is!" The old woman's dark eyes widened, her expression intense. She looked back at the box. "There is one item missing. A ring made of gold and inset with a red stone. I've never seen it. It went missing so long ago that all that is left of it are the rumors that it once existed. The ring is said to be imbued with regenerative power, but who knows?" She shrugged. "The rest of these are tools by which you will use to always protect the clan while you live." She picked up the parchment. "This is the map of this land." She gestured around them. "Our land. We have always inhabited it, and we always will. It is an ancient deed of sorts, an agreement between the Curarya and the original owner, Dragos Anghelescu. It is so old we dare not open it for fear it will crumble. You must keep it inside this box away from the elements." She put it back inside tucking it down between the folds of faded velvet. "This bowl and these oils are used to heal, to summon portents, and to protect. You must use them sparingly because they are all that is left of the essentials brought over from Asia. They were made by Buddhist monks from a monastery in the mountains of Tibet nearly a thousand years ago."

"No kidding around?" Dana's jaw fell. She was blown over by the news she was the next clan shaman, and now these valuable and ancient items were being entrusted to her. She just couldn't fathom it all.

"It is no joke!" Adina scolded her. "Listen carefully, grand-daughter, for all that I teach you is important."

"Yes, ma'am." Dana closed her mouth and sat straighter. She did not wish to offend her grandmother.

"Now," Adina picked up the pendant, "this is a divining stone. The quartz is so old, I cannot say for sure its age, but it comes from the Carpathian Mountains. It works only for those blessed with the gift. Go grab that map over there of the region." She pointed to a travel Atlas on the side table.

Dana got up to retrieve it. She came back, unfolding the paper and spreading it out next to the box on the coffee table.

Adina smoothed out the wrinkles. "These are convenient, and cheap. All gas stations carry them. Remember that." She glanced at the younger woman.

"So, what do we do? She could be anywhere by now." Dana looked at the sheer size of the area from the city to the outskirts and beyond.

"Hold it." She handed Dana the pendant. "You are her friend. You know her, what she looks like, sounds like. Get a clear image of her in your mind. Hold the pendant over the map." She lifted Dana's hand high allowing the chain to dangle. Slowly, she moved her granddaughter's hand creating a circle. The quartz swung clockwise completing a circuit around, again and again. "Picture Meghan. Can you see her in your head?"

"Yes, grandmama. I see her." Dana had her eyes closed. She listened to her grandmother speaking even though she felt kind of silly. Sure, she now believed her about the Strigoi, the feeling that had come over her when she encountered him, but could she believe in this? In magic?

Behind them, Cosmin, Sorin, Stefan, Ilana, Dana's parents, Stefan's parents, and a host of cousins and in-laws all piled in with their children. Dana didn't hear them. She also did not see what they saw.

Sorin stopped, his mouth hanging open. He glanced at his grandmother who gave him a stern look that told him not to speak.

"Now, tell the pendant to find her. Not out loud, but in your mind. Tell it to show you exactly where she is."

Cosmin drew Anamaria to his side. Their two children, Maximillian and Ava hid behind their legs. Young Alexandru stood between Stefan and Ilana. Marius and Renee looked at their daughter, stunned. The rest of the family fanned out in a semi-circle around the back of the couch and chair in awe.

Dana glowed. A reddish light enveloped her entire being as the pendant held in her hand swung around and around with a mind of its own. Even as they all watched, a wide swath of Dana's dark hair began to turn white. It started at the roots and seemed to spill down the length where it ended at her waist. The color that once saturated those strands was leeched out leaving a platinum stripe behind.

The pendant slowed down. It swung away from their property to the center of Bucharest in Old Town. It stopped, hovering, suspended and unmoving.

Adina's brows drew together. "That's odd. I would not imagine the Strigoi would take her back to the university."

"What?" Dana started to open her eyes, but her grandmother's words stopped her.

"Hold, granddaughter. You've seen the vampire. Ask the pendant to locate him."

Dana called up the image of the man from Stefan's tavern. The pendant began to swing once again, glowing a deeper red than the light engulfing her. A sudden gust of wind whipped her hair as the pendant stopped.

Sorin sucked in a breath. Cosmin crossed himself. Adina placed her hand over Dana's and lowered it.

"You can stop now."

Dana opened her eyes, catching the last of the red haze around her as it faded. The smoky quartz swallowed it up pulling it all back into its center. "What is this?" She stumbled backwards against the couch cushions.

Adina took the chain from her granddaughter's hand. She unhooked the clasp as she leaned forward to place it around Dana's neck. Gently, she lifted her beloved granddaughter's hair out from under the links of the chain. Her gnarled hand lifted Dana's chin. "It is your power. This pendant has chosen you." She lifted a strand of the now white hair holding it out for the girl to see.

"Dearest God!" Dana couldn't believe what she was seeing or feeling. The pendant pulsed against her chest, emitting an energy and spreading a subtle warmth through her body.

"The torch has passed. You are now officially the clan's shaman." Adina kissed her cheeks, then backed up and out of the way.

One by one, each member of her family came forth to offer congratulations. Dana looked at them like they had all lost their minds.

Sorin spoke, breaking up the strange moment. "So, what did she find?" He asked his grandmother.

"According to the pendant, Meghan is back in the city, perhaps in her room. I do not know this area." She pointed to the spot on the map.

Sorin knew it. "That's not quite on the campus, but just outside. How did she get there? What in the world would she be doing there on her own?" He looked around.

Adina gave her noncommittal shrug. "That is a good question, but the better question is, why is the Strigoi still here on our land?" She moved her finger and pointed to the southern side of the property close to the river.

"Our families are in the cabins. Are you saying the vampire is over there now?" Cosmin came forward lugging a rifle.

"The pendant doesn't lie. If the Strigoi has come here looking for her and does not find her, he will come after us next."

Cosmin glanced at Stefan. The men in the room all shared a knowing look, each nodding in agreement. Sorin clapped his brother on the shoulder.

"Then we get him first. Come, everyone stay inside. No one leaves this house until we get back. He cannot come in, and Dana can protect you all inside these walls."

"What? Me?" She jumped up, fear in her eyes.

Cosmin gripped her shoulders. "Sister, you are now anointed. You have the power to repel the Strigoi. You must keep everyone safe if it comes to that. Have no fear. Grandmother will guide you." He kissed her cheek. His chocolate-brown eyes took in her appearance. His usually stern, square features relaxed just a bit allowing for a small smile to spread on his lips. "Look at you, all grown up. I am proud of you, Dana."

The moisture in his eyes and the love in his voice touched her deeply. She hugged him tightly. "Thank you, brother. Please don't get killed." She looked at her father, younger brother, and cousin. "None of you are allowed to be killed, do you understand?"

Marius laughed. "If you want us to return in one piece, daughter, then you must bestow your blessing upon us."

Cosmin, Sorin, Stefan, Marius, and the rest of the hunting party stepped forward with heads bowed.

Dana didn't quite know what to do or say, but at her grandmother's nod, she recited a prayer for protection. "Surround these men in light and love, keep them on the righteous path, and shield them with your grace, oh Blessed Virgin. Guide them in your wisdom and deliver them from evil, for they are your humble servants." She made the sign of the cross, and for extra measure, unsure why she even did it, lifted the pendant, closed her eyes, and pictured them all cocooned within the red glow. The room lit up around the group of men briefly before fading away.

Each of them lifted their heads, and a few wiped tears from their eyes. Dana smiled at them. "Now, go catch that bad vampire, and let us find our sister, Meghan, before it is too late."

Mark felt like a sledgehammer had bashed his skull. He tried to move, but his limbs wouldn't respond. He felt as weak as a kitten, which was highly unusual since he possessed supernatural strength. Voices filtered in through the darkness that still threatened to pull him back under.

"Is it strong enough to hold him?"

"It's made with silver and iron. Just lock it into place."

"We need help lifting him. Grab that end and heave on the count of three."

The whole world tilted. Mark experienced a tossing motion akin to being on a ship at sea during a storm. It ended quickly. Another voice broke through.

"I think this is his horse."

"A fine animal," someone replied. "Tie him to the back of the wagon."

The rocking motion began again, but this time, he was sure it was due to the wagon mentioned. He tried to crack open an eye and caught sight of the starry sky through heavy-lidded slits. "Meghan?" he croaked out.

"Be quiet, vampire! You will be confessing soon enough."

The sharp rebuke angered him. He wanted to snap the fool's neck. *Did he know who he was talking to?* He supposed he probably did since the man called him 'vampire'. Still, in his weakened condition, he could do nothing about it—yet.

The lethargy and pain in his limbs had Mark simmering in searing agony. He knew he was surrounded by silver and iron bars, a cage. He was locked inside and unable to break free.

He tried opening his eyes again checking the position of the moon. There were at least three hours until dawn. If they left him outside on the back of the wagon, the sun would kill him. If they tried to carry him into one of the homes without an invitation, that would kill him too. The only good alternative was if they put him inside the barn or one of the work sheds. Both might protect him from the sunlight if he was lucky, and neither required an invitation.

His eyes glanced left and right. He saw only the sides of the wagon. Wooden slats. His ears detected only male voices. His senses, though lacking their usual strength, could not locate Meghan. He reached out with his mind and came back empty. No trace of her. He tried to speak again.

"Where is she?"

A young man around the age of twenty-two or twenty-three peered over at him from the front of the wagon. He appeared strong with a face that would appeal to the fairer sex.

"You will not touch her, Strigoi! She is ours now. Part of our family. She is protected, you understand?"

Mark focused on him, seeing past his features and into his mind. "I would never harm Meghan, Sorin."

Sorin sucked in a breath. "Devil!"

Mark chuckled. "No, not a devil, just a mind-reader. Where is she? She was with me, but I can't sense her. Is she okay?"

Sorin didn't know what to say. He glanced back at Stefan who rode beside him on the bench of the wagon holding the reins of the horses pulling it.

Stefan heard the exchange, and his brows came together. "What do you mean she was with you?"

"We were in the glen. She was about to come back to the house," *I think*, "when I somehow passed out. I don't remember how that happened. One moment we were talking, and the next, all went black. Did you find her with me?"

Stefan pulled on the reins, bringing the wagon to a stop. He leaned over and stared at the vampire in the cage. He'd never seen a Strigoi before. To him, it just looked like a man, but his cousins had warned him that it was simply not so. They also said not to listen to anything it said because evil always speaks to deceive, but what this thing was saying didn't make any sense. If it wanted Meghan, and it had her, how did it lose her?

He looked at his cousin. "Sorin, where, exactly, did the pendant show Meghan to be?"

"Near the university. In Old Town." They looked at each other.

Mark blew out a breath. "Petrescu!" The anger in his voice spiked.

"Another Strigoi?" Sorin looked at the vampire in the cage.

"No. He is not a vampire. He is very human. He is one of you!"

"One of us?" Stefan asked. "There is no one in our clan by that name."

"He is older than all of you, as old as myself. He's a professor at the university, and he wants Meghan. Has always wanted her."

None of it made sense to them. Cosmin walked up and knocked the side of the wagon with the butt of his rifle.

"Stop talking to it! It lies."

Stefan and Sorin jumped.

Mark grunted. "I have no need to lie. I love her. I would never harm her. But someone has taken her, and the only person who could do it, would even consider it, is Peter Petrescu. He is Lovarya, and the thorn in my existence."

Cosmin snorted. "See? Lies! The Lovarya have been extinct as a clan for centuries. They are only stories around a campfire now."

"And yet he is alive," Mark muttered. "While you waste your time with me, he is the one who threatens her life. It happened then, and it is happening again." The disgust in his voice was only partially directed at the gypsy men. Most of it was reserved for himself. Once again, he'd let her down. Once again, Petrescu had taken his woman. He knew it. There was no other explanation, and the monster that lived inside of him was desperate to get out, find the man, and rip him to shreds until only his bloodied, disembodied parts remained.

"If you don't listen to what I am telling you, he will kill her."

Cosmin snarled. "You just said he wanted her, this person. If that is true, why would he kill her?"

Mark locked eyes with the man. He took in the stout build and broad upper body, but it was the pugnacious set to his face that told the vampire this man was not one to be easily manipulated. The fact that he had some difficulty worming his way inside the gypsy's mind showed real strength of will.

"Because she will refuse him, just as she did then. And he will kill her...again."

Cosmin grabbed the side of the wagon, lifting his foot to find a hold on the wheel, and hoisted himself up and over. He stood staring down into the cage.

"You will explain yourself, and then you will tell me where we can find Miss Hartley, or I will leave you in the middle of this field to greet the rising sun."

Mark knew he was serious, but that didn't matter. What did matter was that the man was now listening. He launched into the shortest possible version of his and Meghan's history. All the men had gathered around the wagon. Each stood in silence, taking in his words. When he finished relaying the important facts, the one called Stefan spoke up, having grasped onto a single detail.

"How did you become Strigoi? You said you were on your way to find Meghan's past self, but you did not make it, that you somehow blacked out. Do you not know your maker, vampire?"

The question seemed unimportant to Mark. "No, I've never met him or her. Why is that important? Time is slipping away and here we sit with you asking irrelevant questions!" He spoke in anger, but they ignored him. Instead, each looked at the other, and Mark couldn't break through their thoughts. They'd each thrown up a mental shield. Damn gypsies!

"Get him back to the barn," Cosmin told Sorin and Stefan. "I'll ride ahead with Marius to the house. We need to speak to Dana right away." He jumped off the wagon, landing on the ground. Without a backward glance, he rejoined an older man who stood holding the reins of two chestnut geldings. They mounted and rode off.

Stefan flicked the reins and the wagon rolled. It took fifteen minutes to reach the barn, and another nearly thirty minutes before they could unhitch the horses, leaving Mark in the cage, still loaded on the flatbed. Both walked out, locking the barn door as they went.

He looked around the dark interior. It smelled of hay and manure. There were a few gaps in the wooden slats of the walls, but none he could detect where they left him. *At least I'm covered. Seems they aren't ready to kill me just yet.* He yanked at the iron bars. Steam rose from the contact as the metal burned his skin. He let go almost immediately. *I can't fail you again, Mihaela. Not again.* Mark hung his head low as pain worse than his fresh burns ripped at his soul.

Chapter 11

Dana sat quietly. She'd just heard a long and convoluted tale that made her eyes cross. Next to her, her grandmother chewed her thumbnail in silence. Everyone in the family waited with bated breath to hear what their elder and their clan shaman made of the new development.

"It is possible that the one who made him was destroyed before it could mentor its newest progeny, right?" Dana looked sideways at her grandmother.

"No. If the maker had been destroyed, then this vampire would not have completed the process of turning. This is something else." Adina Lazar Veleru looked at Cosmin. "And he says this Petrescu is human? That he is of the Lovarya?"

Cosmin nodded.

Adina reached for the box on the table. She caressed the worn wood. "There are tales passed down to me from my own grandmama. She told my mother that the gifts we have," she reached over and absently patted Dana on the knee, "came from the most powerful Romani witch ever there was. Her name was Magdalena, or so I have been told. Legend says she was Lovarya, but it was so long ago, there are no witnesses to confirm these stories. Still..."

She sat thinking. "I know that at one time, both clans were at war with each other until the leading families of each clan ended the strife through the marriage of their children. That is how Curarya and Lovarya combined and became one. The ruling and surviving clan is our own because the groom was of the Curarya." She looked up at them all. "If you cannot beat them in battle, marry their women and breed out the enemy. That is what my grandfather used to say."

"Do you think that this man is telling the truth, grandmama?" Dana asked.

"It is possible, but only one way to know for sure."

"How?"

"We must go confront him." Adina stood and pulled her red shawl around her thin shoulders. "Come, Dana. It is time to face your fears."

Remembering the panicked feeling being in his presence caused, Dana stayed seated, her eyes wide, as she beseeched her grandmother silently. Adina would have none of it.

"Stand up, Dana Maria Veleru! You are now the clan shaman. The power that is unleashed inside of you will protect you from the Strigoi. He cannot harm you anymore. Now, you can destroy him with a thought." She pointed at the pendant hanging around her neck. "It has chosen you. It will protect you. Trust in that."

Dana clutched the smoky quartz stone without thinking and it warmed in her hand. "Why did it never choose you, grandmama? You had it in your possession all these years. You've been our shaman. Are you saying you've done it without this power?"

Adina chuckled. It was a deep and aged sound. "My granddaughter, the gifts I possess need no talisman. Come. We go to confront this vampire. We will get our truth, and then we will plan."

"Where am I?" Meghan came to the way the sun rises, slowly, and with increasing awareness.

"My home. Do you like it?"

That voice. She knew it. It had made her skin crawl more than once. Meghan turned her head, looking around the room. It was dark, lit by a dim, single, overhead bulb. The walls were concrete and stone, and she could feel a draft coming in from one of the small windows placed high on the opposite wall. She tried sitting up, but rope kept her tied down on the wide cot that she noticed was chained to the stones behind her. She glanced up quickly, finding the source of the disturbing voice, and glared at Peter Petrescu.

"What the hell have you done? What is this?' She tugged at the ropes binding her.

The man laughed with derision. "Don't fret over that. It is temporary." He reached up to run his hand through his unbound hair, smoothing it back. Squatting down next to the cot, he began caressing her cheek. "I've waited a very long time for this reunion, Mihaela."

Meghan shivered, a bad feeling slinking over her. She jerked her face away from his touch, but this only made him angry. He gripped her chin and forced her to look at him.

"Do not turn from me! You were to be mine, and you will be. Old Magdalena promised I would have a second chance and here you are." His anger seemed to roll in and out like the tide. The glare in his dark eyes subsided as a look of longing replaced it. The grip he had on her chin relaxed as his thumb rubbed her lower lip. "Perhaps this is a better version of you, my sweet. A more modern Mihaela."

His voice dropped to a husky whisper as his face loomed over hers. Meghan wanted to vomit at his nearness, and the madness in both his expression and his words scared the hell out of her.

She needed to keep him talking, try to find a way out of this mess. "What are you talking about?" Meghan tried to keep her tone soft, non-confrontational.

"I watched you," he said.

Her eyebrows rose in surprise. "Watched me?"

"Yes. I watched you give to him what you denied to me." He stretched his fingers out, sliding them into her hair, and twirling the strands around. Petrescu waited for her response, and seeing her disgust, gripped her hair, yanking it painfully until she cried out.

"Stop!" she gasped.

"That's better. An honest response." He smiled. "That is what I like to see from you. But back to what I was saying…" He loosened his hold and resumed playing with her honey-blonde hair. "You play the whore beautifully, you know. It was quite seductive watching you let go, even if it was with that bastard, son-of-a-pig nobleman! He is a monster, Meghan. Did you know that?" He pulled her hair again.

"Ow!"

He leaned down and kissed her open mouth, shoving his tongue inside. Meghan gagged, squirming, and tossing her head to break the contact. He bit her lip, drawing blood, and she screamed. Her efforts seemed only to further amuse and encourage him. Peter pulled back, chuckling.

"Who is the monster, Professor?" She spat.

"I am as human as you, Miss Hartley, I promise."

"That's impossible given what I know." She shot daggers at him with a flash of her eyes.

"Oh, really? And what is it you know, pray tell?" He smiled, bemused.

"I know you're over eight-hundred years old."

He flicked his fingers dismissively, his pinky ring flashing. "A trifling detail, for I have not aged."

"And that you were nothing but an abusive bully to this Mihaela. She didn't want you. She never wanted you. You disgusted her! You disgust me!" The heat of her words felt good in the moment, but Meghan feared they may have been rash.

His expression changed from amused to angry. "You were mine, and he took you! Don't you see? Our families were meant to be aligned. You were meant to be my wife, to bear my children, and all of that was taken by that entitled fool! That is why I made the pact with Magdalena, my soul for you, for revenge on Anghelescu."

This surprised Meghan. He was dead serious, talking about things she'd only ever read in books; fictional books.

"You bartered your soul? Why would you do that?" It seemed absurd.

He softened. "Because I loved you."

"You don't know what love is, Peter. You can't abuse and bully someone and then claim to love them." She kept her tone cautious and light.

He leaned in again cradling her head. "You could have shown me the right path. I would have done anything for you, Mihaela. I would do anything now. Just... love me." He sounded defeated, old, and very tired. His anguish was sincere.

"What happened to Mihaela that night? What did you do to her... to me?" Meghan needed to stall for time, but she also needed answers. Something inside of her was awakening, and she didn't quite know what it was, but it demanded the truth.

The shutters came halfway down as his defenses rose. Despite that initial reaction, Petrescu seemed to recognize what might be his only opportunity to explain himself, to win her over.

"I followed you," he said. "I had been following you for weeks every time you went off to meet with Anghelescu. I watched you with him, always so open, so loving. You never showed that to me." He began stroking her hair away from her forehead, exhibiting an unnerving tenderness. "Your father came to our home; did you know that?"

Meghan noticed he seemed to be confusing her with the person she was supposed to have been so long ago. He really was truly mad, and she was afraid. She shook her head no, trying to remain as calm and quiet as possible.

"Well, he did. Simion came and told my father that the marriage between us was off, no discussions. On what was supposed to be our wedding day! He said your happiness mattered the most to him, and I didn't make you happy, that you'd fallen for the son of our benefactor and landlord, Dragos Anghelescu. He sounded very convincing, but my father had already heard rumors. He knew that the son paid a high price to obtain you, more than my father could afford, and our family was considered rich by Romani standards. When he left, my mother tried to console me, and my father warned me to stay away from you. He said, 'Son, she is no longer worthy of a Petrescu. She's the whore of a *gagiu* nobleman now. She is nothing.' I was devastated, both that you had lost your way, and that, in turn, caused me to lose you."

He sat back on his heels and sighed. "I did not understand what you saw in him. Still, I couldn't stay away. I followed you. I watched you together." A faraway look entered his eyes as he spoke softly. "When he touched you, I wanted to scream." Petrescu ran his hand down Meghan's neck slowly.

She shuddered, feeling revulsion, and unable to lift her arms to slap his hand away.

"When he stripped you down and bared your bounty to the sun, I wept." His hand absently kneaded her breast. "And when you spread your legs to invite him inside, I wanted to tear him apart!" Fingers gripped her soft flesh painfully.

Meghan whimpered, desperate for him to stop. "But what happened the night Mihaela disappeared?"

Her question brought him back to the present and his hand relaxed, but did not budge from where it rested. Instead, he caressed her over her shirt.

"After you both went at it like animals, the two of you began to plan. I listened from the weeds. You were going to leave with him, to run off and marry that night. I could not allow that to happen. When you left the glen, I followed you. I remember it all so clearly, Mihaela," he whispered, drawing closer again. His face was hovering over her own and a mad zeal lit his dark, deep-set eyes. "You looked so glorious in the last light of the sun, like a gypsy goddess as you skipped back to our camp. I wanted to see you like this always, but for me, not for him! I could not let you go, you understand, yes?" His face contorted with remembered pain and his expression begged her forgiveness.

His lips were less than an inch from her own, and Meghan, feeling extreme alarm, nodded. Her eyes reflected her own mounting horror, but he didn't seem to notice. He just kept rambling.

"I came upon you fast. You never stood a chance. I was too strong. I had to have you. I had to make you mine, to show you how I..." He sucked in a breath, staring down at her mouth, and then his thin lips descended. He kissed Meghan, who protested, turning her head this way and that, but he locked his large hands around either side of her face and held her still.

"Do not fight me again, Mihaela. Do not!" He plundered her mouth, and it made her sick. When she tried to bite his tongue, he pulled back, laughing before kissing a trail down her neck to her chest. He let his hands roam freely touching her everywhere, dipping between her thighs as his fingers dug into her, pressing hard. Panicked, she screamed.

"Stop! You killed her, didn't you? You fucking rapist! She didn't love you! I don't love you! Stop it, stop it, stop it!" Meghan shouted her words and thrashed as much as she could manage in her bindings. The cot shook with the force of it all, and the shrill tone of her voice finally seeped into his sick, passion-addled brain.

Peter stopped and looked at her. He appeared confused. "Don't say that, Mihaela. Please, don't deny me. I'm so sorry I was too rough. So sorry I broke your... your beautiful neck." He was breaking down. A tear fell from his eye, landing on her chest. He caressed her neck absently.

Meghan knew this man was cracking up before her eyes, and the danger of that was very real. She had to keep him talking.

Someone would come for her, wouldn't they? Mark! Mark said they were psychically connected. She concentrated on him in her mind. *Mark! Are you there? Can you hear me? Petrescu has me. I'm in his house, down in the basement. He's going to kill me. Help me, please!* "Inside her head, she was beyond panicked, but outwardly, she tried to be calm. If she stayed cool, Petrescu might stay calm too. It was her only chance.

"What happened after... you killed her?"

He wouldn't look at her then. He sat back quietly, breathing slowly.

Finally, "I carried your body to the witch." Peter began absently turning the ring on his finger around and around. "I begged her to bring you back, but she said even she was not powerful enough to restore life to the dead. I lost my mind. I attacked the crazy old woman, but she stopped me with her magic." He laughed. "Tossed me across the room like a rag doll, like I was nothing. I begged her to find a way, any way to bring you back to me. She said there was only one way, and it would only happen if the powers that be granted it." He looked at Meghan. "She said I must wait for your soul to come back in the form of another. She said I would know it was you."

Shaking her head, Meghan held her breath, afraid of what he would say next.

I hear you! Meghan? Are you still with me?

Meghan's eyes grew wide as she heard the voice inside her head. She caught herself reacting and shut it down. The last thing she wanted was for Petrescu to realize she was communicating with Mark. *Yes, I'm here. Please hurry, Mark. He's out of his mind!*

Keep him talking. I'm trying to find a way out myself. Your damn gypsy family have me caged in the barn. Wait! I hear them coming. Keep him talking. Try not to do anything to anger him. He enjoys causing pain, specifically, hurting you.

Mark's words weren't anything she didn't already know.

Meghan kept her eyes on Petrescu, but in her mind said, '*He's telling me what happened then. He killed Mihaela, Mark. He killed her... me. Said he did it after she left you in the glen, after you... we made our plans. This is damn confusing! He took her body to the old clan witch, Magdalena.*

Meghan could almost picture Mark shaking his head, and she certainly felt his anger.

As soon as I get out of here, I'm coming to get you. And Meghan?

Yes?

I'm going to kill him.

She couldn't think of anything else to say to that. Meghan didn't advocate killing anyone, but if it came down to her life or Petrescu's, she chose her own. He'd killed her once already, and once was enough!

Peter continued talking. "Little did I know you would look exactly like yourself. I waited for a sign, and with each passing year, lost faith. That damned old woman. I fell for her tricks. She demanded payment from me. She demanded my soul. In return, she gave me this ring," he held out his hand, "and said I must never remove it. It would give me the longevity I needed to wait for your soul to reincarnate."

Meghan looked at it. Now she knew why it seemed delicate. It was a woman's ring. "What will happen if you remove it?"

He pulled his hand back to his side and stared at Meghan. "I will age again and die, I believe."

"But aren't you sort of dead already? I mean, you have no soul, or so you say." Her innocent question incensed him.

"I have no soul because I gave it up for you, woman! Don't you understand? I have given up ever living a normal life, of ever knowing peace in death, all for you!"

She gasped. "I didn't ask you to do that, and neither did Mihaela. You made that choice. Why did she want your soul? What did she do with it?"

A sadness entered his troubled eyes. "She absorbed it. Claimed it as her own. I think my soul gave her greater power."

"But if she had a longevity ring, didn't she already have great power? She could have lived forever.'

"Yes, she could have, but you see, the old witch had no soul of her own. I didn't realize it until after I made the bargain. She'd already lived for centuries. None of us knew exactly how old Magdalena really was. She was an old woman when I was child, and she looked exactly the same when I was a grown man. So, you see, I was convenient in my desperation. She needed a willing soul, and I was more than willing. She needed a soul because to die without one means the person burns in hell for all eternity with no chance for redemption. And we all, even the worst of us, have a chance for redemption. That is why souls reincarnate. It's another chance to get things right."

Meghan thought about that. It was so metaphysical, so strangely Zoroastrian and new age that it blew her mind. "So, after you completed this deal…"

"She removed the ring, put it on my finger, and that was that." He looked down at the piece of jewelry with disgust. "Except for the other part."

"What other part? What else did you do?"

The sly glance he tossed her way sent chills down her spine. "My grief was not assuaged as you can imagine. I had just doomed myself to waiting for God knew how long before you showed up again. It was all his fault. Had Anghelescu not interfered in our family's arrangement, none of this ever would have happened. The old woman told me I must be the one to kill her. That is how she obtained the ring and the power, and so it should follow, that is what I must do. She was desperate to die. I didn't understand that then, but I do now. Centuries of living alone, never having family or love or friends is a torment all its own. I told her I wouldn't do it, not unless she granted me one last favor."

"Mark." Meghan knew it would be bad.

"Yes. Marku. I denied the biddy her peace lest she help me get my revenge. She gave me a weapon, one she cursed with death. All I had to do was drive it into his flesh. With her help, he never saw me coming, and I must say, it was very satisfying to stab him in the heart. When I left him, he was dead, just as she told me he would be, but wouldn't you know it, that wicked bat cursed him not to permanent death, but living death. I returned to our village and Magdalena asked for one day to get her affairs in order. I was happy to grant the wish since part of me was satisfied. I didn't have you, but Anghelescu was dead. I didn't have you, Mihaela," he reached out to hold Meghan's hand, "but I knew I would one day. She promised. Still, like all deals made with the devil, mine backfired. Imagine my surprise the next night when I was supposed to take Magdalena's life, your lover showed up. He tore through our camp killing everyone. He killed my mother, my father, your family, our friends. He was a monster! I ran and never came back. For the first hundred years, I kept my eyes upon his family, always from the shadows. No one would admit it, but it was clear something wasn't right. When old Dragos Anghelescu died twenty years later, a young *'nephew'* showed up to lay claim to the land. I caught sight of him, and sure enough, it was Marku. The estate kept getting passed down to a descendant, always a young man who came around after thirty to fifty years. By then, no one remembered him. He was just a relative. He stayed on or near the land, never straying far. I've known he was out here for some time, a walking dead man like myself, and yet not like me."

In her mind, Meghan relayed everything Petrescu was telling her. She felt the rage rolling off Mark, but he kept his composure.

Don't lose faith, Meghan. Do you trust me?

Meghan thought about it, and she realized she did trust him. Nowhere in their story, then or now, had he harmed her. He could have, but he never did. Certainly not when they were human eight hundred years ago, and not now when he was cursed to be a vampire. All he'd done was love her. She smiled. *Yes, I trust you.*

"Nothing to say? I killed your lover, cursed him to vampirism forever, and you go quiet. Why?" Peter studied her face.

Meghan looked at him. "I'm tired, and thirsty." She licked her lips.

Petrescu watched the motion, smirking. "Well, you've had quite the night, haven't you?" He twirled a lock of her hair. "It doesn't matter now. You're here!" He swooped down, dropping a hard, fast kiss on her lips. "I will get you some water, and then we have plans to make." He stood.

"Plans?"

He smiled down at her. "Yes, we are to be married finally." Petrescu's smile widened to a self-satisfied grin.

Meghan panicked. What if Mark didn't make it in time? She couldn't marry this lunatic. "Mark will come for you, Peter." She threw out the only threat she could think of.

His smile disappeared as he shook his head. "No, Mihaela, he won't. The sun will be up in a few hours and there will be nothing left of Anghelescu. I left him unconscious. Undisturbed. The powder will keep him that way until it is too late for him to escape the dawn." He leaned over her, his hands resting on either side of her head, a smirk on his thin lips. "Accept your fate. You are mine." He left her then, walking to the stairs and taking them two at a time up to the first floor.

Alone in the basement, Meghan prayed Mark would find a way to rescue her before it was too late. If, indeed, the sun was going to be an impediment, she would need to figure something else out. Her father taught her to think and to be independent. The gears in her mind began to spin. The answer lay somewhere in his story.

Chapter 12

A small army of angry gypsies walked into the barn and surrounded the wagon. Each stared at Mark as if he were some alien creature. He'd already met a few of them, but he was now confronted by what he detected was a very powerful old witch, and a new development, a powerful new witch.

He stared at Meghan's little gypsy friend. When he first laid eyes on her inside the tavern, she appeared so small, so frightened, and easily intimidated. He could smell her blood and knew her for what she was then, but this woman who now stood before him seemed taller, stronger, and perhaps, wiser. The telling white streak in her hair marked her in the old ways. As a child, Mark remembered his own mother telling tales of travelers imbued with the power of the elements. That was where witches drew their strength, from nature. Most were unrecognizable as witches or shaman because they possessed the power of only one element. But those blessed with command over all of nature, they were marked with a lock of white hair.

The old woman next to her gave off power, but all of her hair was a dark gray, so Mark couldn't quite tell if she was a witch of one element or all. But Dana Veleru clearly inherited all, and recently.

The old woman stepped forward. "You will tell me what I want to know, Strigoi!"

Mark suppressed a smile. She actually reminded him of his old nanny who was also Curarya. Angelina raised him until he was twelve, and from then on, he was sent to train with his father's men in arms, and to ride the land learning the family business. Angelina had been tough on him, but always with a loving hand.

"What do you want to know?" A small curl of his lip escaped him making his cheek dimple.

"What have you done with Meghan Hartley?" She pointed a bony finger at him.

"Nothing."

Her eyes widened at his reply. "You lie! She was taken from her bed inside my home!"

Mark sat up and looked her straight in the eye. "I did not take her. She came willingly. And I have not harmed her. She was taken from me by an old enemy, one of your own as a matter of fact. His name is Peter Petrescu."

"You dare to talk back—" she began.

"Grandmama, hold." Dana stepped forward. "How do you know of Petrescu?" Although Cosmin had already relayed the story, she wanted to hear it from his lips. He could not lie to her. She knew this. The pendant sent assurance through her that it would know if he lied.

"Peter Petrescu is a filthy, gypsy dog—"

"Watch yourself, vampire!" Cosmin raised his shotgun and aimed.

Mark toned down his rhetoric. "Petrescu is of the Lovarya. They lived on this land eight hundred years ago. He is as old as I am, but he is not Strigoi. He is human. I couldn't believe it either when I saw him. He is the same man responsible for the death of my beloved." He looked at Dana. "She is the young woman you know as your friend, little gypsy. Meghan Hartley is the reincarnation of my Mihaela. We were to be married when I was still human. In all honesty, I did take her from him, but only because he was an abusive bastard, and it was her choice too. We fell in love. It is as simple as that. Now, I have her back, and damned if he didn't take her again." He gripped the bars, smoke sizzling as the iron and silver burned his hands. "And he will kill her again if you don't let me out of here!"

No one spoke. Stefan's eyes nearly popped out of his head seeing the smoke. He crossed himself, stepping back. Sorin aimed his rifle at the vampire from the opposite side. They weren't taking any chances.

"How did you become Strigoi?" Again, the old woman addressed him.

Mark sighed. It seemed they would grill him and waste time. "I don't know, Adina Lazar Veleru."

She sucked in a breath and narrowed her eyes. "Parlor tricks! You will not enter my head again or I will crush you!" She made a fist and squeezed.

Mark felt his neck tighten painfully cutting off his airway. It was a good thing he didn't actually need to breathe, but he did need his throat open to speak. He held up his hands in surrender.

"Okay, okay." He composed himself. "I answered you honestly. I don't know. I was riding my horse to Mihaela's camp. She'd gone missing and I was determined to find her. I had suspicions that Petrescu had taken her. I never made it, not that night, at least. Something happened. I was riding along, and then I was down, and all went black. When I woke again, it was the next night, and the transformation was under way. I slaughtered my own horse. My thirst was so great that I continued to kill, drinking in the blood of my victims. I took out nearly her whole tribe, and through my red haze, I still searched for her. I never found her. I never found Petrescu, either."

"And you never met your maker, the one who turned you?" she asked, clearly astonished.

"No, never. I was on my own from that night on. I couldn't return to my own family. I feared I would kill them, kill my own mother and father." He sat back on his heels, careful to avoid the bars of his cage.

Adina looked at Dana. "You see? This is not normal. This is not the usual way."

"No, it's not. And I finally know why." Mark pulled their attention to him.

"What do you mean?" Dana asked.

"Meghan," he began. "She and I are connected, here." He pointed to his head. "Don't hate me, but I did bite her. I have partaken of her blood."

"I knew it!" Adina shouted.

"It's not what you think, old woman. I love her! I could easily kill her, and yet I have done no such thing. I invited her to join me tonight, to show her the place where we used to meet once upon a time hoping it might somehow unleash ancient memories. I don't know." He looked lost, disgusted with himself. "Anyhow, my link to her has built up over the last few weeks between entering her dreams to get to know her again, and sharing our bodies tonight."

"You did what? That is a breach of a woman's boundaries, vampire!" Dana was incensed.

"Mark. My name is Mark, or rather, Marku Andrei Angehelscu."

"I don't care!" she said.

"Wait." Adina stopped her granddaughter. "You said you have the psychic link with her?"

"Yes, that's what I'm trying to tell you. She called out to me. She's at Petrescu's home. He has her tied up in his basement.

Apparently, he's in a confessing mood, thinks I'm about to die as soon as the sun comes up. I'm sure that was his plan."

"We may still let it happen. Don't get too comfortable," Cosmin added.

"So, what has he confessed?" Adina spoke.

Mark looked up at her, weariness as old as time on his face, and rage in his eyes. "He is the reason I am a vampire. When he killed Mihaela, he made a bargain with some old gypsy witch named Magdalena to give him long life and ensure he would find her again. He also cursed me to this living hell."

Adina gasped. "Did you say Magdalena?"

"Yes, that's what Meghan said. I met her once, on that first night as I was transforming. I tried to kill her. She very nearly killed me." He half-smiled without a hint of humor.

Adina grabbed Dana's hand. "The ring. She gave him the ring!"

"The one you mentioned earlier?" Dana grasped her pendant.

"Yes." The old woman stepped closer to Mark, mere inches from the cage. "What does it look like?"

"I haven't seen it. I don't know."

"Ask her now. Ask Meghan." She waited.

Mark closed his eyes and concentrated. After a few minutes, he opened them again. "She said it's gold and has a ruby inset, that it's a woman's ring. She also confirmed what you said about the witch giving it to him."

Adina closed the gap between herself and the wagon. She reached up and wrapped her thin, bony fingers around the cage.

Mark watched her, unmoving, with the eyes of a predator waiting to strike.

"How would you like to be human again, Strigoi?" she whispered softly.

Her words struck him dumb. His attention shifted as shock filled him. "What are you saying, old woman?"

"I am saying that the ring is the key. It was cursed. Any longevity Magdalena gave to Petrescu, any curse upon yourself, all of it is connected. The ring was her power, and when she gave it up, it became his. Anything he did with it after the transfer of the ring, any act of violence or attempt to curse you came from him. If he thinks Magdalena created the curse, it was a ruse, one to serve her own purpose."

"Meghan said the old witch wanted to die, so she absorbed Petrescu's soul."

"Yes, but she could not die by her own hands. It needed to be by his, and his alone. Otherwise, she still lives. Did he kill her?"

"She was still alive when I went into the camp that night. Petrescu was gone. I don't know."

"Humph. If the pact was not complete, then Magdalena still lives, and it can be undone. The ring must be destroyed. Doing so will reverse all. Petrescu's soul will be returned. You will be healed of your vampirism. You can be human again… if you wish it."

Mark felt something move in his chest. It had been so long since he'd felt his own heart beat that the emotion simulating the effect startled him. *Human? Is this possible?* Joy filled him. The idea that he could once again walk in daylight as a man, at Meghan's side, thrilled him. All he needed to do was get the ring, but for that to happen, they needed to get him out of this cage.

"And what if the pact was completed and we still destroy the ring? What then?" He asked.

Adina shrugged. "Then nothing... for you. But it will be death for Petrescu."

That's good enough for me. "You will have to let me out. The sun will be up soon, and I cannot function in daylight. I can help, but only tonight. You need to lure Petrescu out of the house, rescue Meghan. I will do the rest."

Adina stared at him as did they all. Distrust was written all over their faces.

"You can trust me. I won't hurt you. Don't you know what you've just offered me? My life back! Even if that were not the case, rescuing Meghan is the priority. I cannot live with myself if something happens to her again. Please!"

Sorin nudged his sister. "Does he tell the truth?"

Dana held the pendant, standing quietly. She waited for a signal, some kind of sign, but all she received was a steady energy. The quartz stone was calm. The vampire's words had not set off any alarms. "He does." She looked at Cosmin and Stefan. "Release him."

Stefan took a step back, fear on his face. Cosmin glared at Mark.

"I will not harm you. You have my word as a gentleman."

"Know if you do, I will shoot you. And if that doesn't work, she," he pointed at Dana, "now has the power to destroy you. You understand?"

Mark sighed. "Yes, I understand." He moved to the back of the cage to allow them to feel safer while Cosmin stepped forward with a key. Stefan kept his eyes on him the entire time as he pulled the door open standing behind it. They all looked like they were setting a wild animal free, one that might run off, or might turn on them at any moment.

Mark crawled out, careful to avoid the bars. When he cleared the cage, he hopped down off the wagon. Everyone around him jumped back. He tried not to chuckle. "I'll need my horse. Please bring Dracula to me."

"You named your horse Dracula?" Sorin asked, laughing in astonishment.

"Yes, I know. It's ironic." Mark smirked.

Stefan went to the back and led the black stallion out of the corral. "The saddle is there." He pointed to the far wall where it hung over a sawhorse.

Mark retrieved it, and quickly hooked the saddle and reins. He'd never done so with an audience before, but they stayed, watching his every move. When he was finished, he swung himself up onto the beast's back. Dracula snorted and stamped his hooves, ready to run.

"No funny business, vampire. Remember, if you wish to be human again, you will show up as soon as night falls. We will be ready." Adina dressed him down without fear. Mark smiled feeling more human already as memories of similar admonishments from his old nanny bubbled up. He liked this old witch, even if she didn't trust him, and would as soon kill him.

"I won't let you down, dear lady. You've given me a precious gift, something I haven't known for centuries. Hope. Oh, and please get used to calling me Mark. *Vampire* is so derogatory." Before he left, he rattled off Petrescu's address, and he relayed what he knew of the lay of the man's house to Cosmin and Sorin. Then, creature of the night and impatient beast rode off. The sky was already growing lighter, but they flew like the wind. Mark grinned. This might be the very last time he fell away dead to the world as soon as the sun came up. His joy was immense, but he knew it all hinged on the gypsies rescuing Meghan and hopefully capturing Petrescu. Even if they didn't get him, and all they had was Meghan, the gypsy dog would come for her, and Mark knew he would kill the man with great pleasure. It would be over soon either way.

"Fly, Dracula, fly!" He whipped the stallion's haunches.

Meghan was in hell. Petrescu had returned with a glass of water, and had stayed. Worse, she had to endure the unmitigated humiliation of him walking her up the stairs to the bathroom while she was still tied. He held the end of the rope like a leash and would not even allow her any privacy. He both undressed and redressed her after she relieved her bladder. Then it was a march back down the stairs where he secured her to the cot once again.

"I will need to leave you for a few hours, just to prepare for our wedding, my love." He'd come back from the kitchen with toast and some juice that he tried to feed her. Meghan was having none of it.

"I am not marrying you, Peter. I don't love you." She said it for what felt like the millionth time, and as with each time before, her words fell on deaf ears.

"But, of course, you will. We are meant to be." He leaned down and kissed her cheek. "I've waited so long for this," he whispered. "Behave while I am gone, Mihaela. Remember you cannot get out of here. Even if by some miracle you escaped these knots, the basement will be locked. Just rest up. Tonight is our honeymoon and I expect you to participate fully." He stood and left her there, mouth agape.

It was quiet once she was alone. Meghan tried to reach Mark in her head, but he wasn't answering. She wondered if perhaps Dana's family had killed him after all. If that was the case, she would be next because there was no way she was going to let Petrescu touch her anymore. He'd already violated her enough. If the worst case presented itself, she'd go down fighting, even die, before going along with his sick plans.

She felt tired. Bone tired. The exhaustion of the past several hours, the uncertainty, the fear, all took its toll. A tear slipped past her lid and trickled down her cheek. She knew she should be trying to find a way out of her bindings, but her mind felt numb. All she wanted to do was close her eyes. Soon, her body decided for her.

A bang and a click warned her he was back. Meghan tensed. She felt like she'd only just closed her eyes. Had she slept that long? She turned her head, straining to look up at the stairway. Footsteps came down slowly. A figure began to enter her field of vision, tall, strong, and handsome.

"Sorin?" Her voice squeaked.

"Meghan!" He ran to her, a shotgun in his hands as he sighted right and left.

"He's not here. He left, but he'll be back shortly." She struggled to sit up.

"Here, let me..." Sorin pulled a hunting knife from his boot and cut through the ropes.

Meghan could finally move her arms. She threw them around Sorin and began to cry.

"Sssh, now. Don't cry. We're here. We're all here." He held her tight even as he helped lift her to her feet. "We have to get out of here."

Cosmin, Stefan, and Dana all came down the stairs.

"Did you find her?"

Meghan caught sight of her friend and ran to her. Dana wrapped her arms around her, and at Cosmin's urging, they headed up the stairs. Adina was at the top, waiting.

"Come, child. We must get you to safety." She grabbed Meghan's hand and pulled her along. They left the house, going out the side door, and ran down to the sidewalk where Stefan's hippie van waited. Ilana was at the wheel.

Meghan climbed in and her tears fell. They'd come for her, all of them... except for Mark.

"Dana, what happened to Mark?"

Dana still had not let go of her hand. "Don't worry, my friend. He is safe. He will be at the house tonight. Petrescu will come for you." Her face grew serious. "This is not over."

"I know, but where is he? Why can't I reach him?"

"He is vampire, Meghan." She pointed out the window. "It is daylight. He is dead to the world until the sun goes down."

Meghan stopped. She hadn't even thought of that. It still seemed unreal that all the folklore she'd ever heard about vampires seemed to be true. It was then she noticed her friend. Reaching out, she picked up the white lock of hair spilling down Dana's shoulder.

"What happened?"

Adina looked across at the girls. "She has come into her power. Meet the new shaman for the Veleru clan." The old woman smiled with pride and patted her granddaughter on the shoulder.

"I seem to have missed a great deal." Meghan was in awe. When she and Dana had gone to bed the night before, she was a sweet, rather naïve mathematics teacher. Now, her whole demeanor had changed. There was a maturity and wisdom to her that had not quite been present earlier.

"Much has happened, it is true. We will tell you everything once we get back to the house. For now, you look exhausted." Dana put her arm around her friend. "Rest, Meghan. You will need all your strength to finish this."

Meghan wanted to argue, to ask more questions, but her eyes felt heavy. She felt safe for the moment. Funny, she thought. Hadn't Petrescu basically said the same thing only a little while ago?

"Okay, but you have to fill me in. And I have a lot to tell you too."

"We know." Dana patted her friend's head.

The motion of the van on the bumpy roads, and the secure feeling of being surrounded by people who'd just risked their lives to rescue her, lulled her into a stupor. Drowsiness set in, adding weight to her eyelids. They closed, and the ride back was peaceful. That ended all too soon.

"Meghan, wake up!" Dana shook her friend's shoulder roughly.

"Wha...?" Meghan cracked her lids open and then immediately lifted her hand to shield her face from the mid-morning sun. It burned, and it felt like someone had thrown sand into her eyes. The van wasn't moving. "What is it? Why are we stopped?"

She sat up, shaking her head to clear the cobwebs. Ilana was as still as a statue behind the wheel. The motor still hummed, but they were not moving. Stefan sat next to her with his mouth hanging open. In front of her, Cosmin stared straight ahead muttering to himself and making the sign of the cross. Sorin was already sliding the side door open and stepping out with his shotgun raised. Dana edged closer to Meghan, but it was Adina's face that caught her attention. The old woman looked stunned. She was staring straight ahead at the road. Meghan followed her line of sight and there, standing in front of the van was a very old woman. She was hunched at the shoulders with long, flowing white hair. Her stature was small, but the hand she held out in front of her glowed with a bright, red light.

"What the hell is that?"

"I don't know, my friend." Dana gripped her hand.

"She just stepped out in front of us, and then... the van stopped." Cosmin whispered, his voice filled with unease.

"It is her." Adina's voice shook.

"Who her?" Meghan asked.

"Magdalena," she rasped.

"What? *The* Magdalena? As in, the witch Petrescu bargained with?" Meghan sat forward, staring. She turned suddenly to Dana. "He told me he made a deal with her to bring Mihaela back, but when she couldn't, the bargain was re-struck with him being granted some boon of meeting back up with her again, er... with me. Anyhow, she gave him a ring that supposedly holds the power of immortality, and in return, he gave up his soul. I can't believe I'm saying this. It sounds ridiculous."

"Yes, yes. We already know this. Your vampire shared the story." Dana turned to her grandmother. "What does she want? Why is she here now? How is she even here now?"

Adina looked past Dana to Meghan. "She is here for you."

"Me? I don't even know her!" This was so far beyond sane that Meghan just couldn't comprehend it anymore, and she was sick of it.

"It does not matter that you don't know her and do not fully believe." She turned her focus to Dana. "Remember, child, when I said that the deal between them was never completed? He failed. Petrescu failed, and now," she looked back out at the road, "she is here to make sure the deal is done. She will use Meghan to get what she wants."

"And what the hell does she want?" Meghan had lost all patience.

"Death!" The reply came from the old woman on the road. Everyone gasped.

"Dear sweet Virgin, she can hear us!" Stefan, who'd sat frozen, squeaked.

"Send her out!" She pointed a gnarled finger at Meghan.

"We can't just let her go, grandmother. We can fight!" Dana clutched her stone. It was glowing red.

"Do not try it, shaman. I am more powerful than you and your elder put together, and I have no desire this day to kill my descendants." Her voice was strong despite her obvious age.

Meghan looked around at each of them. In a very short time, she'd grown fond of these people, and in that same amount of time, she'd put them in danger. It was time to face this on her own. It seemed no one could help her but herself. Somehow, this whole situation was tied into her personal destiny. Only the original players could finish it.

"Move aside." She began climbing over Dana.

"Meghan, no!" Dana tried to hold onto her hand, but she shook it off gently.

"It's going to be okay, Dana. I don't think she wants to kill me."

"No, she does not, but Petrescu does," Adina answered.

Meghan moved past Dana and stepped over Adina, stopping to give her a quick, tight hug. "Thank you for trying to help me. It means everything to me that you accepted me into your family."

The serious look in Adina's eyes melted away to sorrow and compassion. "I only wish I could have done more, child." She suddenly wrapped her arms around Meghan and whispered in her ear, "Your vampire can be saved. He can be human again, all can be reversed, but only if the ring is destroyed. Do not let her complete the pact if you can stop it."

Meghan pulled back and stared, her eyes wide with shock.

"I do not have all day!" The ancient woman barked.

Sorin helped Meghan out and onto the road. He'd been nothing but kind and brave. She reached up and pushed his dark hair out of his eyes. "Thank you, Sorin. Keep them safe." She kissed his cheek, and then with one last wave at Stefan, Ilana, and Cosmin, she walked forward to Magdalena, to greet her destiny.

A wrinkled hand snatched at her own, and in the blink of an eye, they disappeared from sight, leaving behind the passengers in the VW van rolling forward once again. All were stunned by what they'd just witnessed, and all grieved the loss of the young woman their clan adopted.

Chapter 13

The curtains automatically opened, but Mark was already bounding out of bed. Night had fallen and he was eager to discover if the gypsies had been successful. He reached out in his mind to Meghan.

Are you there? Meghan?

There was no answer. He tried again with the same result. Nothing. That was odd. Even if she'd been sleeping, he should have been able to get through to her. He dressed quickly, and bypassing saddling Dracula for transportation, took to the sky instead. He flew straight for the Veleru compound.

If the old woman was right, and there was a possibility to reverse the curse, therefore ending his vampirism, this would probably be the only thing he'd really miss. There was nothing like it. Being free from the rules of gravity, having the ability to take to the sky and move like the wind was its own special kind of magic. He knew he would love to share this with Meghan, but if all went according to plan, there wouldn't be time. Mark was okay with that since there were a million other things he could share with her should he become human again, like breathing, and growing old.

He laughed. The idea of his heart beating once again felt like an even greater miracle than flying. *The things I took for granted! The sun on my face, feeling temperatures, even catching a cold.* He smiled. *Having children...* The possibilities were endless, and he knew he would trade away this supernatural existence for fifty, thirty, even twenty years of humanity with the woman he loved. This was his second chance, and he was not going to let anything, or anyone stop him from grabbing it with both hands and claiming it for himself.

He sighted the cluster of houses and descended. Landing atop the roof of the main house, he climbed down with the joy of a small boy on Christmas morning. Mark stood before the front door. suddenly apprehensive. He straightened his clothes, ran his fingers through his windswept hair, putting it in order, and slapped his own face several times with his hands. If the fates were kind, Meghan was inside, and Adina Veleru either had Petrescu or the ring, or a way to get both figured out. The most important of those was Meghan's safety. He forced air into his lungs and reached out, knocking on the massive wooden door with three solid raps.

The door swung wide. Cosmin stood with a shotgun raised and aimed at his chest.

"Woah!" Mark stepped back, hands raised.

Cosmin lowered the barrel. "Oh, it's you." He looked outside checking left and right. "I thought it might be the other bastard."

Mark eyed the man. "You didn't get him?"

"He wasn't there when we arrived."

If his heart could plummet in his chest, Mark would be experiencing terrible anxiety at that moment. "And Meghan? Please tell me you found her?"

"Yes. We found her." Cosmin's voice did not sound happy.

"But?" Mark asked, afraid of the answer.

The older man sighed, then pointed a finger at Mark. "There is much to tell you, but I am not inviting you inside unless I have your word as a gentleman, one who has the chance to be human again," he reminded him, "that you will harm no one in this house, not ever! If you do, I swear to the Virgin, I will cut out your dead heart myself!"

Mark recognized both how serious this man was, and how much faith he was placing in him by even considering the offer to invite him inside. It was a dangerous and risky move which meant only one thing, Meghan was in serious danger, and they were desperate.

"You have my word." He extended his hand in the age-old gesture of trust among honorable men.

Cosmin eyed the hand like it was a snake about to bite him, but then he lifted his own hand, spit in it, and gripped Mark's, shaking it once with strength before saying the words. "I invite you inside, vampire."

Mark took the hint. Although they'd just made a deal as men, the gypsy reminded him he was aware that first and foremost, he was Strigoi, and Cosmin wouldn't be forgetting that fact anytime soon.

The gypsy backed up, and Mark walked inside wiping his palm on his pant leg. He followed to the living room where everyone seemed to be waiting. He looked around the room at every face. Hers was missing.

"You said you found her?" He cast a sideways glance at Cosmin.

"We did."

"So where is she?" Anger edged Mark's words.

Dana Veleru stood up. The power rolling off her now commanded his attention. It seemed to have grown since that morning, and might continue to do so. The little gypsy, he noted, was going to be one formidable witch.

"You will calm yourself, vampire."

Her words washed over him, and his anger faded.

Dammit! I need my edge. "Then explain to me, please," he added politely, "how it is she is not here?"

"Sit," she said.

Mark's feet moved forward carrying him to the chair opposite the old woman. He didn't like that his body responded to her command without his own permission. She must surely have the abilities of a necromancer. This was not something he cared for at all. He sat.

"We found Meghan this morning, and we even got her out of Petrescu's home." She paced back and forth. "We were on our way back here when we were ambushed in the mountain pass."

"By whom?" *Who the hell could have possibly ambushed a vanload of gypsies?*

"Magdalena." She stopped pacing and stared at him.

"What? Are you kidding me?"

"Do I appear as though this is some kind of joke?"

Mark took in the seriousness of her expression, the sincerity in her dark eyes. She wasn't joking. She truly meant that the old witch, from eight-hundred years back, had somehow ambushed them... and taken Meghan?

"But why would she take Meghan, for that is surely what you're trying to say?"

Dana sighed. She glanced at her grandmother. The old woman cleared her throat.

"It seems I was correct in my speculation. The original pact was never completed. Petrescu was supposed to kill her, but with his desire to curse you and bring you harm, and your blood-thirsty transformation, it all went wrong. Or perhaps Petrescu never meant to honor his end of the deal. I am not quite sure, but it was, indeed, Magdalena, my ancestor. She is determined to complete the transaction. She wants to die, and the only way it can happen is if the person whose soul she absorbed ends her life. She took Meghan to lure Petrescu to her. She will hold her ransom, offering her only in exchange for her own death."

"And all of you together could not stop one decrepit old woman?" Incredulity oozed out of Mark's mouth. "What about you?" He looked at Dana. "You are becoming more powerful by the hour if I am any judge. Are you saying you couldn't take her?"

"Yes, that is what I am saying."

"You weren't there, Strigoi. You did not witness what we saw with our own eyes." Cosmin spoke up. "She stopped the van in its tracks with one flick of her wrist."

"And she could hear our conversation inside the vehicle although she was standing out front in the road." Stefan threw in his two cents.

"You said it yourself, Anghelescu." Adina turned his attention to her. Mark noticed she did not call him vampire or Strigoi. "She is over eight-hundred years old. She has had nothing but time to increase her own power. What she gave to Petrescu when she handed over that ring was nothing to what she already inherited through her own blood. She is more powerful than Dana, and far more powerful than myself. She would have crushed us all because she is desperate to end her existence. You, of all people, should understand the monotony and loneliness of immortality."

He did understand, but that didn't change the fact that he was furious, and felt helpless. "So, what are we to do?"

"She wants Petrescu. You want Meghan. If he is still at his home, then the only chance you have is to secure him. Make a trade."

"Then what is everyone waiting for?" Mark stood up.

"We were waiting for you."

"And what about what you said this morning, about reversing the curse. Is that still possible? You said this woman is too powerful to defeat."

Adina nodded. " 'Tis true. The stakes are high. It is up to you what you feel you can risk. If the ring is destroyed, Petrescu's soul will be ripped from her and returned to him. At that moment, he will be completely mortal, and therefore, you can kill him. But stripping the soul she needs in order to die from her body will not diminish Magdalena's powers. It might temporarily weaken her, but she can still kill you for it."

Mark paced. "And if I let her have her way, allow Petrescu to kill her?"

"Then he will still be immortal, and you will not be able to kill him. He will forever be a threat to you and to Meghan. Also, you will not ever again have the chance to become human."

He ran his fingers through his hair, clearly frustrated. "Those are not good odds either way."

"No, they are not," she said.

Mark thought over everything she'd said, everything he remembered Meghan telling him. He turned to Adina swiftly. "Wait, you said the ring keeps him immortal, that he must wear it at all times. What would happen if I can get the ring off his finger?"

The old woman raised a dark gray eyebrow. "He would age and die... without a soul."

"And be condemned to hell?" Mark's lips spread in a gleeful smile.

"Yes."

"Could I then destroy the ring?"

"No. The pact would be complete, and your vampirism, permanent."

"Dammit! My choices to save us both are few." He sat back down and chewed his thumbnail. It was a very human thing to do. Sorrow entered his eyes. "There really is only one way forward, the only way to save Meghan. I must get the ring from Petrescu and destroy it."

Ilana, who'd sat quietly throughout the conversation, gasped. "But the old witch will kill you!"

Mark looked at her. He remembered her from the tavern. She was lively, and kind, and always smiling at her patrons. He'd witnessed the love between her and Stefan, had seen how happy they were as a family, having their son working in the family business. At the time, it hadn't moved him, but it did now. It was what he wanted more than anything else in the world for himself and Meghan. But it was not meant to be. The only way to save her was to sacrifice himself.

"Yes, she will, but not before I kill Petrescu. I need someone with me, someone to be ready to get Meghan out of wherever the old woman is holding her. Once she's killed me, she will have had her revenge. I'll make sure of it."

"How can you make sure she doesn't come after Meghan, after us?" Sorin eyed Mark with skepticism.

"Because gypsies love deals, and I'm going to make her an offer she cannot refuse." Mark quoted from his favorite movie, The Godfather.

"What deal? What can you offer an eight-hundred-year-old witch that will matter to her? All she wants is to die." Sorin stood, hands on his hips.

"Sorin, you let me worry about that." To Dana, he said, "Do you think maybe you can slow her down a little, give me enough time to end Petrescu?"

Dana knew she would be in the direct line of fire if she did, but her friend's life was on the line. "Yes."

"Dana, no!" Adina stood up abruptly.

"It's okay, grandmama—"

"Silence!" Adina shouted. "You will not risk yourself. You are the next shaman for this clan. You are needed here." She lifted her hand and spoke three ancient words in rapid succession. Dana froze and began falling sideways, drifting off to sleep. Sorin dove and caught his sister.

"Take her up to her room and lock her inside, Sorin. I am ordering you to stand guard over her and this family." She turned to Cosmin. "You will come." Then she looked at Stefan. "And you will help get Meghan away." She returned her attention to Mark whose mouth was hanging open slightly in surprise. "I will slow her down. No arguments, Strigoi!" She pointed a bony finger in his face.

Mark threw his hands up in surrender. "No argument from me, madam." Part of him wanted to smile. She couldn't have reminded him more of his nanny Angelina in that moment if she tried. Forceful, stubborn to a fault, and fiercely protective of those she loved. He understood, too, what she was thinking. She was old, and if things went south, her life was already near its end. She would not let her children or grandchildren suffer in her place. She would face the enemy, and he could see she was a force of nature, an opponent even old Magdalena herself would respect.

Cosmin's eyes were wide, and his expression, thunderstruck. "I did not know you could do that, grandmama."

"You have seen nothing yet, grandson," she promised.

Mark stood. "Well, let's go get Petrescu then."

Cosmin was still in shock. Stefan kissed Ilana, and then walked to his cousin, giving him a small slap across the face. "Snap out of it. I'll drive."

Adina shocked Mark by putting her arm through his. It had been a long time since anyone had trusted him near, and even longer since he'd played the gentleman. "You'll need a coat, dear lady. I believe it is cold outside." He picked up the thick, gray, shawl-style coat off the peg in the hall as they passed. He stopped and placed it around her shoulders. If he wasn't mistaken, she smiled just a little. The entire family watched his kind act, and no one could believe it. The Velerus would be telling this story for generations to come—the night a Strigoi came into their home and was tamed to gentleness by their tiny, yet all-powerful grandmother, Adina Lazar Veleru.

"So how long do you plan to keep me?" Meghan sat on a wooden chair next to a rickety, hand-built table made from old crates in a room carved out of the side of a mountain. By her best guess, they weren't that far from the Veleru compound. Apparently, Magdalena had not strayed too far from the home she always knew.

"Until the pact is complete, child." She sat near the fire upon a three-legged stool. It didn't look comfortable at all, but it was surely warmer.

"And then what?" Meghan had watched the old woman from the moment they arrived just outside of the cave opening. It appeared as if the energy Magdalena had expended to stop the van and transport them to her home had drained her. She was listless and a little grumpy.

"Then, he can have you." She didn't seem to care.

"It doesn't bother you at all that I don't want him, that he will kill me?" Meghan had a difficult time believing anyone could be so callous.

Magdalena turned her head slowly, her eyes, buried in wrinkles, found hers. There was nothing there. "No. Your life is fleeting. If he kills you, you will go through purgatory, and then onto the next life, the next lesson. I envy you. It will always be fresh and new. As for me, I don't even know what I could possibly gain from reincarnating. I've already lived hundreds of lifetimes in one body. All I want is peace. All I dream of is oblivion." She turned back to the fire and hunched further into her shawl.

"Maybe you can learn compassion for your fellow man." Meghan stated blithely.

The old woman chuckled. "You have spunk. And maybe you will figure out how to get away from Petrescu on your own."

"Sure. Perhaps Mark will kill him. He's the only one up to the task as far as I can tell with the powers you've given to Peter making him strong and immortal."

A spark of curiosity lit her dull eyes. "And who is this Mark?"

Surprised, Meghan asked, "You don't know? The vampire you helped create that night you made the pact with Petrescu. He asked for your help to kill a man. Don't you remember?"

The woman's head cocked to the right, and then she opened her mouth and began to laugh revealing the few teeth she had left. It was raw and hoarse, and creepy.

"What's so funny?"

Magdalena tried to get herself under control. It took a moment as a few more belly laughs shook her frail body. Finally, she took a deep breath and spoke.

"I remember he wanted revenge against your lover. I remember that once I absorbed his soul and felt its rot, I was angry. Do you know what a petty, small, and spiritually crippled man he is? No? I can tell you that I was desperate for a soul, any soul, but my desperation brought me the worst possible candidate. His is a black soul, but there was just enough good in it to give me what I needed, if only I could die."

"Petrescu had some good in him?" Meghan sounded skeptical.

"Yes," she said, her face growing serious. "He had honest feelings for you. Oh, not all of them, but their origins began when he was but a boy, and those were the ones based in purity. It was a small boon for me, but a boon nonetheless. That was to be my ticket to the purgatorial realm. I would gladly suffer every moment of pain he caused in life for that one chance of redemption in the end. That is what purgatory is, Miss Hartley. You go there and visit all those you harmed in life. You feel their pain, and you learn your lessons. When the review is complete, you move on and choose your next life, your next set of lessons. The goal is to always evolve and grow as a soul to obtain both enlightenment and god-like purity. It is only when we have learned all lessons that we can ascend to the highest realm, that of the all-soul itself—the place where souls are born, and the place they return for eternal peace."

Meghan stared at her. That was way more information than any human should have. It was far more than the human mind could comprehend. She focused on something less complicated.

"But what about Mark?"

"Ah, yes. I knew Petrescu's soul in that moment. I knew he might renege somehow. He lacks integrity. When he begged for my help to gain his revenge on your lover, I cursed a dagger and told him he would need to plunge it into the man. It would guarantee death."

"But he isn't dead." Meghan was confused.

"Isn't he? He is the living dead. I know. I saw him. He came to the camp the next night, wild with anger and bloodlust. He came searching for you." She pointed at Meghan. "I did not know his name then. Mark, you say?"

"But why would you do such a thing? It has been hell for him, and he was a good person!" Indignation whipped up like a storm inside of her.

"Child, what is done cannot be undone, at least, not until we all come together again. The dagger that I told Petrescu was cursed with death was... cursed with his own death." She laughed at her own inside joke.

Meghan didn't get it, as was clear by the expression on her face.

The old woman continued. "You say your lover will come for Petrescu, and I say death comes for him. You see, I had to ensure my own revenge should the pig not follow through on his own promise. If Petrescu would not give me what I wanted, I made sure to deny him what he wanted more than his own soul. Your Strigoi is the weapon of Petrescu's death. He holds the power within himself to accomplish the task, my power in the form of his strength. It transferred through the wound. Blood sealed the spell. And once he puts that rabid dog down, he will be free of the curse." She looked down and muttered, "Funny, I thought he must have met his own end long ago. I truly despaired I had lost my chance at revenge. I figured the Strigoi would have found Petrescu before now, and when I kept sensing the liar's existence, thought someone else had staked the vampire or maybe he did not love you as much as he implied." She shrugged her shoulders, muttering.

Meghan tried to process this information. Her eyes widened.

"Yes, my child, human once more. But I must have my own end first." Magdalena stood, her legs unsteady. "I need to die. Please, understand." She beseeched her.

Rising from her chair, Meghan searched the old woman's eyes for any hint or clue she might not be telling the truth, but all she saw was weariness. If this was true, then Mark could become human, but he would have to kill to do it, and what would that cost his own soul?

"I see you thinking. Yes, he would be killing another, but Petrescu is outside of the eye of God without his soul. His death would not be a stain upon your lover's own."

"If that's all true, then he needs to know." She didn't know why, but she did not want to reveal she could mentally communicate with Mark, even though she couldn't seem to reach him since her arrival in Magdalena's home. Something was blocking her attempts and she suspected it was the old woman. But why?

Magdalena's eyes shifted. "He will know when the time comes. We will all be present."

Meghan noticed the shift. "How did you know where to find me?"

The wind began to pick up outside, gusting into the recesses of the cave. The fire flickered in the pit. Darkness was settling in, but there was a darkness inside the cave that had the hair on Meghan's neck standing up as goosebumps popped up all over her skin.

The old woman stepped closer. "I harbor his soul. I am connected to the soul's source at all times. I know what he feels, hears, and sees. I've known of your reappearance since he first became aware of it." She smiled, but it was not pleasant to behold. "And he is aware of me. He will know where to meet us. I've already sent the message. This will end, finally, where it all began."

Her heart was pounding in her chest. "When?"

"Soon."

Now Meghan could confirm that the woman was shielding them somehow from the outside world because she all but admitted to communicating with Petrescu in basically the same way she, herself, could communicate with Mark. The dangerous old woman was orchestrating her own death, or so she said. Still, something wasn't right.

"You traded your own soul for that ring, did you not?"

"I was tricked!" Magdalena shouted. "The one who gave me the ring did not tell me the details of our bargain until he was dying... by my hand! Yes, I felt something had happened. I felt then as if my essence had been ripped from my body, painfully. He said I would be giving myself as a gift to save him from damnation, that it was an unselfish act... of love." She whispered the last two words.

It hit Meghan then, and her eyes widened. "You loved him. He was your love."

"And he betrayed me. Damned me!"

The two women stared at each other. Young woman and old crone. Understanding flowed between them. Meghan reached out and took Magdalena's frail, wrinkled hand. "You have lived all these centuries alone because the man you loved betrayed you. You know the pain of betrayal twice over because Petrescu failed to follow through and end your life. I get it. I'm so sorry, Magdalena."

Old eyes looked down at Meghan's hand on hers. She was clearly uncomfortable with being touched. She tried to pull her hand away, but the younger woman's gripped tightened just enough to hold on. Meghan leaned down and hugged her.

"No one should be left alone."

A sound disturbed the quiet. It began as a sharp intake of breath, and rolled into a deep, hoarse sob. Magdalena's frail body shuddered with pain. Centuries' worth of tears slowly poured out of her eyes and rolled down her face, getting lost in the rivulets of wrinkles wrought by time.

"Sssh. You're not alone anymore." Meghan pulled back a bit and looked at her. "Did you know that Mihaela was Lovarya? If I really was her, and you were the village shaman, then that makes us family. I am your family, Magdalena. You're not alone." She wiped away tears even as moisture blurred her own eyes.

The old woman continued to cry, but she no longer pushed Meghan away. She held on tight, letting her loneliness and pain wash away. "I am so sorry, child. I have helped doom you to this."

They stayed that way for what seemed an eternity, two women holding onto one another while the wind howled, and the moon rose in the night sky. Finally, they separated. Magdalena held Meghan's hands, sniffing back the last of her tears. "The time is almost upon us, and now I don't know what to do. I do not want to put you in danger."

"I know what to do. We're going to find your peace. We're going to finish this, and I am going to be there to hold your hand until the end." Meghan smoothed the old woman's hair back. "Once peace has found you, I will make sure Petrescu never gets to enjoy his full power. You're sure that Mark can kill him?"

"Oh, yes. He has access to my power, and it is far more than that of what Petrescu will enjoy with the ring. I have no doubt your Strigoi will be successful. Fate has brought you back, but not for that dog. Fate has brought you back for your chance—for his chance—to love and be loved." She looked bemused by the thought. "There is no love in Petrescu. To love, one must have a soul."

"Then it's decided. I'm ready whenever you are." The two women locked hands, and in a blink, they were gone. Outside, the wind continued to blow, moaning its sorrow to a cold and starless sky.

Chapter 14

The van rolled to a stop a block down from Petrescu's home. As they were about to get out, Cosmin stopped Mark.

"Wait! What's happening?" He pointed at the house.

The garage door ascended. Taillights glowed red as the car inside began to back out.

"Where is he going?" Mark asked out loud.

"We will follow him." Adina patted Mark on his knee. "Magdalena will waste no time. Wherever he goes, it is where we need to be."

Mark looked at her like she'd lost her mind. The plan was to secure Petrescu and ransom him to Magdalena. If he failed in even one step of their carefully laid out plan, Meghan could die. He wasn't going to let that happen.

"I'm sorry, but that's not good enough." With a speed their eyes couldn't capture, Mark flung open the door and was gone in a blink.

"What the hell?" Cosmin's neck swiveled around looking right and left, and then back at Mark's empty seat.

He pulled the door closed. Adina spit out a curse. "Impatient man! He is going to get her killed!"

Only Stefan remained calm. "I would have done the same thing," he muttered.

"What are you talking about, Stefan?" Cosmin stared at him with one eyebrow raised.

He turned to look at his cousin. "If it were Ilana, I would have done the same thing. He loves her, or had you not noticed?" He threw looks at them all.

Cosmin countered. "If we deviate from the plan, Meghan could die."

"If he prevents Petrescu from going to meet the old witch, she could still die!" Adina shouted.

Everyone looked ahead as the car backed out into the street. A mist formed and seeped into the window on the passenger side.

"I take it that was him?" Cosmin asked. No one answered, and they turned to Adina.

She shook her head. "It is possible. I have heard stories..." She watched as the car began to rock.

Inside the other vehicle, Peter Petrescu blinked rapidly as smoke filled his car. He reached to unroll the window further and felt a hand grab his neck. He tried to scream as his eyes took in the slowly solidifying form of Marku Anghelescu.

"What? Aren't you happy to see me, gypsy?" Mark grinned evilly at the man, but the grimace disappeared quickly. "Where are you going, Petrescu?"

Peter began to fight. He tugged and clawed at the hand around his neck to no avail. Mark punched him in the face with his free hand.

"Answer me!"

Petrescu's hand gripped the arm wrapped around his neck. Mark glanced down, catching site of the ring.

"That is a rather womanly ring you have there. I had no idea you were so dainty, Peter. Let me have a closer look." Mark pulled the hand away while maintaining the grip on his neck. Petrescu struggled, panic written all over his face. The vampire held the hand up to the light. He studied the ring. "It is rather nice. Perhaps I should take it as a gift..." He let the words trail off as the man's struggles renewed.

Petrescu managed to squeak out, "No!"

"What's that? You're talking now? Good. Tell me where to find Meghan." Mark eased his grip just enough so Petrescu could talk.

"You fool! If you don't let me go, the old woman will kill her. She already warned me."

"Magdalena. Yes, I know about her. Is that where you go now?"

Petrescu nodded.

"Then drive. And if you make one false move, I will kill you myself." The threat was very real.

"And you will lose Meghan!" Petrescu tried to gain leverage.

Mark glared at him, still applying the choke hold. "If Meghan dies, she will be reborn, but as I understand things, you won't, and I will thoroughly enjoy ripping your body apart."

Petrescu's eyes widened. It was clear he was surprised that Anghelescu knew this, and more surprising, seemed willing to let it happen.

"I'm going to release your neck, gypsy. You will drive to wherever it is you are supposed to go. When we get there, I will be taking Meghan. Whatever your business with the old witch, that is on you." He deliberately withheld very important information, namely that he knew exactly what Petrescu's business was, and that he would not live to see it completed. Mark sent a silent message to Adina.

Follow us!

Inside the van, Adina gasped. The message was received loud and clear. She was surprised no one else heard it.

She reached out and smacked Stefan on the back of his head. "Drive! Follow them!"

Nearly an hour passed as one dark Audi and one brightly colored hippie van wound through the mountain passes near Mark's home. He looked around and then realized where they were heading; the ruins to the east of his house. Eight-hundred years ago, that was the site where the Lovarya camped each year. It was where Petrescu's and Mihaela's people lived. It was where Magdalena had lived as the respected clan shaman, and where it all began. All the original players would be back in the same spot, standing on the same soil where the evil bargain was struck. That is where it would all end.

"I suppose it has a sense of completion," said Mark. The ruins on the land were of stone homes that came long after Mihaela's time, and still, they were ancient, slowly being consumed by the earth and eaten alive by all its flora and fauna.

The night sky was black as pitch. A chilling wind whipped through the leaves in the trees, and the waning moon shone overhead offering the only light available outside of car head-lights. It didn't matter to Mark who could see as well in the dark as humans did in daylight.

"Park over there." He pointed to a dirt path halfway over-grown with weeds.

"She is going to kill us all, Anghelescu! She told me to come alone." The anger in his voice didn't faze Mark.

"Get out of the car, Petrescu." Mark waited until the man opened his door and stepped out before joining him. He looked back and didn't see the van, but he sensed them. They were a short distance back. He detected their footsteps with his sen-sitive hearing. Good. The plan was once again back on. Kill Petrescu, and then offer his own life, what little there was of it, in exchange for Meghan's. He hoped it would be enough to appease the witch for what he was about to snatch away... her one chance at death.

Peter looked around. He was agitated and angry. He twisted the ring around his finger glancing around the crumbling buildings searching for Magdalena and Meghan. He knew if he completed the pact, his soul would be lost forever. To date, he'd lived in a sort of limbo, without his soul, but with a slim chance of getting it back. The old woman had betrayed him when Anghelescu didn't die. He had not forgotten, and now the man was here once again to take away his prize.

The trees rustled as the wind grew stronger. It blew debris up from the ground flinging it around them. Mark stood stalwart while Petrescu tried to shield his face. It died down as suddenly as it began, and standing in the middle of the cluster of deteriorating stone homes were two women, one tall, strong, and beautiful, and one shorter, hunched, and frail.

"I see you brought company," the aged one stated.

"I had no choice," Petrescu glanced at Mark, glaring at him. "He invited himself."

Magdalena laughed. "Of course, he did. It is as it should be."

Meghan's eyes found Mark's. Joy sprang up in her heart. She tried to mentally communicate, but she could not get through. She tossed a frustrated look at the old woman.

"So, what is it you want, Strigoi?" she addressed Anghelescu, clearly amused.

"I'm here for her, to secure her safety." He continued to look at Meghan.

"Ah, yes. Love. But you cannot secure her safety. Only he can save her." She pointed at Peter.

Petrescu sneered. "And only if I complete the pact. Only if I kill you. Well, you wicked old hag, you can plainly see you went back on your word." He pointed at Mark.

Magdalena nodded. "Because I knew you could not be trusted."

Peter growled and leapt forward. Mark saw him go for the old woman and moved fast up behind him. He reached for Petrescu's neck intent on snapping it. The world froze.

Mark tried to move, but his limbs would not obey. Petrescu was standing mid-step, unmoving. He rolled his eyes and saw Meghan still standing across from them with her mouth halfway open as if she was trying to shout. Only the old woman moved. She ambled over to Mark slowly, a smug smile on her wrinkled face. When she reached his side, she lifted her hand and patted his arm.

"Be at peace, vampire. I am not going to harm you. But it is time for my end, and I cannot let you take that from me." She stood on her tiptoes, stretching her short body as far as she could manage, and whispered strange words in his ear. He understood, but as soon as he did, his consciousness faded. Everything stopped.

"Mark, no!" Meghan yelled.

Mark hesitated, standing still. Meghan was shaking her head at him, telling him to hold back. What? Why? Petrescu walked ahead of him unharmed. He came to a stop in front of the woman.

He watched in astonishment as his love wrapped her arms around Magdalena, holding her tight. She leaned down and spoke low in her ear, but Mark heard her.

"I'm not going to leave you. It's okay." She kissed the old woman's cheek.

Petrescu's face showed his surprise and confusion.

Magdalena smiled. "Do it now. I am ready"

Peter's hands reached out on their own volition even though his mind was screaming *'Don't do it! You will lose your soul forever!'* His hands gripped the old woman's head and twisted hard to the right. Her frail neck snapped, and her body slumped to the ground. She lay there, broken, a peaceful smile on her face.

Petrescu, now free from a compulsion he never saw happen, threw back his head and howled,

"No!"

Mark's feet rushed forward, and his fangs extended as his eyes glowed amber in the darkness. He descended upon Petrescu like a swarm and sank his teeth into the man's neck. Peter reached back and tried to pry him off, but it was too late. The vampire's teeth drained him of life even as his fingers loosened the ring from his grasping hand. As soon as it was separated from Petrescu, his body slumped to the ground. Mark pulled away and stood back watching as the body of his nemesis aged in seconds, drying up, his cracking into a million pieces that shrank and flew up into the wind like ash, blowing away. Within moments, Peter Petrescu was no more.

Meghan stood in shock, her mouth working, but no words escaping.

Adina, Cosmin, and Stefan came out from the shadows. Mark turned on them, and then stopped, realizing the vampire that resided within was visible by the horror reflected on their faces. He struggled to force it back down inside. Meghan had seen him like this. She'd seen his monster, and he couldn't undo it.

He backed away, fearing he might still hurt her or one of the gypsies. Blood-red tears streamed from his dark eyes. "I'm sorry. I don't know what happened."

Adina pulled her shawl tight and strode toward him. He continued to back away. "No, dear lady. Please don't get too close." He turned his face away even as he stumbled backwards.

"Give it to me, Anghelescu. Hand over the ring. It must be destroyed."

Mark looked at it. It was still in his hand. He handed it over to Adina and turned away. "My chance, it's over. She should never have seen that. She won't be able to forgive me."

Adina held the ring, shaking her head sadly. "You were supposed to kill him first. Now the pact is complete. I cannot speak for Meghan. She may not be able to accept you like this. What can you really offer her anyhow?" Adina spoke only the harsh truth, but her eyes conveyed sympathy.

Mark felt unbelievable pain in his chest. He couldn't look at Meghan who stood ten feet away staring at him in horror.

"Tell her goodbye. Tell her... I tried, and I will always love her. Tell her to be happy." Mark risked one last look at Meghan before turning away and taking to the sky.

The men crossed themselves as they watched the vampire fly away. Cosmin pulled himself together and wrapped his arm around Meghan, leading her away from the old woman's body which was decomposing rapidly. Soon, there would be no evidence at all that two people had come to violent ends within the ruins.

Adina placed the ring atop the remains of a stone wall bordering one of the ancient domiciles. She stood back and began chanting. The ring lit up, and the glow grew brighter. Heat poured out from its core, and the stone set within the gold exploded. The metal melted, seeping into the stone. Absorbed into the rock, the longevity ring was destroyed.

Exhaustion showed on her face. "Let's go home."

Chapter 15

Meghan cried all the way back to the compound. Words would not form. Magdalena had promised her Mark would turn back human once Peter was dead, but what she witnessed was not human. She'd trusted the old hag, had offered her compassion, and even held onto her until the end. She been betrayed. Anger engulfed her, and her heart was broken. He'd left without a word. Just flew off.

Flew off!

When they arrived back at the house, a furious and anxious Dana came running out, Sorin on her heels.

"Meghan! Oh, my goodness." She hugged her friend, overwhelmed and relieved, and helped her inside, throwing looks back at her grandmother. Her eyes promised, *'We'll talk later'* even as they roamed her grandmother assuring herself that she was okay.

"What happened?" Sorin ran to his brother's side.

"Magdalena is dead, so is Petrescu." Cosmin sounded tired. They all were. No one had slept, and each had witnessed things no person should ever have to see.

Stefan was greeted by Ilana who hugged him so tightly, he could barely breathe.

"Where is Alexandru?"

"He's asleep," she said. "He tried to stay up, but I made him go lie down. He was out as soon as his head hit the pillow, poor thing."

"I need to see him, need to hold him. Come with me." He tugged her hand, and they disappeared inside.

Sorin looked back at the empty van. "And the vampire?"

"He is still a vampire. I do not think we will be seeing him again." Adina spoke low, not wanting Meghan to hear her words. If the girl knew there was any chance at all that Anghelescu could have become human again, and that somehow, they had all failed to make that happen, she would be more devastated than she was already. She didn't need that burden on her heart. "Do not say anything to Meghan."

Sorin glanced Meghan's way, then nodded to Adina.

"Let's just get inside, get cleaned up, and try and get some rest. All I want is to be with my wife and children." Cosmin helped his grandmother inside and up to her room.

Everyone found their way to their beds. Dana led Meghan up the stairs. She helped her undress, and even bathed her after filling the tub with hot water. She dried her friend afterwards and slipped a warm, flannel nightgown over her head.

"Come, Ilana prepared you some soup." Dana walked the grief-stricken, silent woman to their room. Inside, Ilana had left a tray with a hot bowl of chicken soup and a glass of juice.

Meghan tried to eat. Her stomach was growling, but her heart wasn't in it. She managed only a few spoons-full and some sips of the cool orange juice before laying down on the bed. Her eyes were gritty from all the tears, and her body was numb. She closed them as Dana pulled the cover over her. Reality slipped away and she was soon sound asleep.

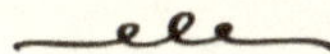

Stefan loaded up the van. Ilana and Alexandru climbed into the front, and Dana and Meghan into the back. It had been an emotional goodbye with Adina.

"Thank you for helping save me."

Adina cupped Meghan's cheek and smiled. "You are welcome, my child. You're one of us now. We are your family." The old woman hugged her fiercely. A sad chuckle shook her small frame. "I do remember what it was like to be in love. My Julien swept me off my feet, and I would not trade one single moment we shared for all the world." She leaned back and looked at the younger woman. "Someday, you will find that love, and even then, you will not regret your short time with Anghelescu. I was wrong. He was not a bad man, merely the victim of another man's twisted vengeance. He did love you. He told me so himself, but he did not need to. His actions proved it. Remember that, Meghan. A man is only as worthy as his actions, and your vampire's showed the very depths of his love for you, and the goodness of his heart."

Moisture sprang into Meghan's eyes, blurring her vision. She sniffed and tried to smile. "Thank you, Adina. Thank you for not telling me I was wrong."

"Love is never wrong." Aged fingers pinched her cheek. "Now, it is time to get back to school. You and Dana will take care of each other, yes?"

"Yes, we will. She's my sister now." Meghan grinned at her friend.

"Let's go already!" Stefan shouted from the van. He shook his head. "Women!"

Ilana reached out and smacked him on the back of his head. "Hush, husband. You love us, admit it."

Cosmin and Anamaria, Sorin, their parents, Marius and Renee, and the rest of the clan stood outside waving goodbye. Meghan climbed into the back of the van followed by Dana. She still couldn't get over the change in her friend. Dana seemed to have grown into herself nearly overnight. And the white streak of hair tucked back into her bun still amazed her. There was such a confidence about her now that Meghan knew the staff and students would not fail to notice.

Stefan cranked the engine, and they pulled out of the driveway heading back to the city center and to the university. For Meghan, it felt like going back to another world, one without Mark, without the man her heart silently cried for.

"What is it, Meghan?" Dana watched her friend's face, noting the faraway look in her eyes.

"I just don't understand, Dana."

"Understand what?"

"She seemed so sincere. I believed her." Meghan looked down at her hands resting in her lap.

"What do you mean? Believed her about what?"

Meghan continued to look down, twiddling her thumbs. "She said Mark was the weapon she made to destroy Petrescu, that she never trusted him to follow through, so when she helped him with his revenge, it was her own revenge she was plotting. She said she transferred some of her own power into Mark and that when he succeeded in killing Petrescu, he would be human again. But that didn't happen. I saw him afterwards. So did Stefan. He was anything but human."

Dana remained quiet, thinking.

"Dana?" Meghan looked up.

"What did you see?"

Meghan shuddered. "Mark killed Petrescu. He bit him." She stopped and tried to gather her thoughts. "It was crazy, like something out of a movie. He pulled the ring off Professor Petrescu's finger, and his body just dried up and blew away." Horror settled into her eyes.

"So, your vampire did not actually kill him, it was the removal of the ring?"

"I suppose so."

"Was this before or after Magdalena's death?" Dana continued to question her friend. They had not spoken of the incident, trying not to dredge up the horrible events.

"After. Mark was with Petrescu when we arrived. Petrescu attacked Magdalena. It was then that he killed her. I stayed with her, Dana. She was a sad old woman, you know?"

Dana sat up and turned, facing Meghan. "You mean to tell me that your vampire just let Petrescu walk over and kill the old woman? He did nothing to stop him?"

Meghan shook her head, concerned by the confusion in her friend's eyes. "No, why?"

"Why?" Dana looked at Meghan, then reached over the seat and smacked Stefan on the back of his head.

"Ow!" He reached back to rub the spot.

"Turn the van around. We must go back!"

Ilana stared at her, alarmed. Stefan began to protest, but Dana was not having it. "Do as I tell you. Turn around and go back!"

"Dana, what's going on?" Meghan's voice rose.

"Why did you not tell me this, cousin?" Dana ignored Meghan and berated Stefan.

He shrugged, glancing over his shoulder at her as he cranked the wheel to make a U-turn. "What? Why does it matter?"

Meghan tried to keep up with the flow of conversation going back and forth between English and Romanian.

Dana rattled off her answer so quickly, it was difficult for Meghan to comprehend. "Because, fool, that was not our plan!

There is no way Anghelescu would have simply stood by and let Petrescu kill the old woman. It would complete the pact. Why did he not kill Petrescu first?"

"I do not know!" Stefan shouted. "We were not close enough to interfere. He did stand there. We all saw him, but did not understand what was happening. The Strigoi did not strike until after Petrescu snapped the old witch's neck."

"Dana, what does this mean?" Ilana asked, worried.

"It means the old woman had you all spelled." Dana looked at Meghan once more. "She told you that if Mark killed Petrescu, he would no longer be vampire?"

"That's what she said, and I believed her. She told her story, of how she came into possession of the ring. She was betrayed by the man she loved. Dana, I saw the truth in her eyes. She lived all these long years with the pain of that betrayal. That was why she didn't trust Petrescu, why she made sure he would die. Come to think of it, I believe she may have been trying to not only protect me from him, but to protect anyone else from ever being tricked into trading their soul to him."

"I am right! I know it." Dana slapped her knee. "Hurry, Stefan!" She was smiling.

Dreams plagued Mark's rest. He tossed and turned as visions of each death he ever brought about ran through past his inner eye. He felt all of their terror, pain, and even sorrow over the lives they lost at the bite of his fangs. He was tormented. Sweat poured from his body as whimpers of apology tried unsuccessfully to burst from his lips. The sleep paralysis would not let it happen, keeping him trapped within its tight hold. Meghan's face was the last one to appear, and with it came peace. Love flowed through him mingled with the pain of regret at having to let her go.

Tears squeezed through his closed eyes. Awareness of the wetness on his cheeks made Mark reach up to wipe the moisture away. He cracked his lids and glared at his fingers in the dark expecting to find them covered in blood. He couldn't see. It was too dark.

"What the hell?" He reached over for the remote control on his nightstand. Finding it, he hit the button for the lamp over his bed. Light flooded the enclosed area blinding him momentarily. When his eyes adjusted, he looked at his hands again. They were clean. Mark blinked and rubbed his eyes again. Still, his fingers came away wet... and clean. He got up, throwing his feet over the side of the bed. He sat there wondering why the blinds had yet to open.

Has something happened to my timer? Dammit!

He stood, naked, and pushed the plush red velvet bed curtains aside. His eyes searched for the old, bronze clock on the mantle above the slate-stone fireplace.

"That can't be right!" He walked to the clock. Mark picked it up and held it to his ear. The tick-tock, tick-tock sound assured him it was still wound up. It was still working, but the clock read 11:42... a.m.

He turned and headed for his desk. Pulling open the computer, he eyed the time.

11:43 a.m.

"What in the world?" He stepped back in shock. If both clocks were correct, there was no way he should be awake. A chill ran over his skin as discomfort crept up from the bottoms of his feet. They hurt in a strange and unfamiliar way. Mark looked down and didn't see anything different about them than from any day before, but he still kept shuffling from one foot to the other. They were uncomfortable. They were... cold? His brow pulled low over his eyes. The feeling of the cold stone on the bottom of his feet was both foreign and somehow familiar. He hadn't experienced cold in eight-hundred years.

Another feeling hit his bladder, and between the chill on his skin and the urgency demanding his immediate attention, he turned and made his way quickly to the bathroom where he utilized the commode for probably the first time ever—for this purpose anyway—and not the once-a-day flush he gave the toilet to keep the pipes flowing. He'd had the bathroom modernized over the years, updated periodically, for no particular reason other than his insane need to at least appear human. Now he stood before the porcelain throne in the thoroughly normal stance of a man taking a morning piss. It seemed to go on forever, and it was the most oddly pleasurable feeling.

When his bladder was finally empty, Mark leaned forward, one hand on the wall, smiling. *What just happened?*

He flushed away the dark yellow urine. Stepping back, he moved back into the bedroom and jumped. Something moved to his right. He spun around ready to take down whoever it was—a very large intruder—and came face to face with himself! There was no intruder. Mark stared in wide-eyed shock at a reflection he had not seen in so long he almost didn't recognize his own face.

"Dear God!" He moved closer, peering at the tall, muscular, hardened man he had become. His hair was on the long side. His eyes held fear and wonder. He looked exactly as he had the very last night of his human life. He reached out and touched the image, awestruck.

Spinning, he ran to the windows, and hitting the manual switch on the wall, stood off to the side, out of the way of the light slowly seeping into his room as the metal shades rolled back. He peeked around, careful not to let the light touch him, and with the caution of one who did not wish to get burned, stuck his finger out to the very edge of the light.

Nothing happened. It didn't hurt.

He extended the finger further until the tip was fully in the direct line of the rays. It did not burn. Mark edged his whole hand in front of the window. He waited, expecting it to burst into flames, but nothing happened. It just felt...warm, nice.

Taking a deep breath—*Breath!*—he stepped fully into the sunlight. Warmth enveloped him, and he did not catch fire. Not even a hint of smoke. He laughed.

"It worked!" Tears fell from his eyes, catching on his long lashes. Laughter bubbled up out of him. He dropped to his knees as emotions overwhelmed him.

"Meghan. Dear God, I must find her!" He got up and turned in circles, unsure what to do first. "Calm down, Anghelescu! Just... shower!" He snapped his fingers. "Yes, shower first."

Mark ran for the shower where he reveled in the heat and steam. He took far longer than he meant to simply because it was the first time he actually felt the water on his skin. He finished up, dried himself, and chose clothing. Once he was dressed, he grabbed his wallet and searched for his keys. He didn't drive often, but he did own a car. He simply usually either rode Dracula or flew.

"Dracula!" Mark kept to a schedule usually, but he'd barely had time to check on the stallion when he got home, and he was certainly in no mood after what happened, thinking all had failed. He walked to the stable across from the house. Dracula heard him and lifted his head, snorting in surprise.

Mark grinned. "Hey, boy!"

He rubbed the horse's nose who snuffled his hand, smelling him. Dracula whinnied as if trying to say, *'You smell different'*.

"I know, but it's a good thing, I promise." He opened the stall, letting the animal out. Mark led him to the side door that opened onto the fenced-in field. He loaded a fresh bale of hay into the outside feeder and turned on the hose to fill the water trough. After he made sure the animal was eating, he mucked out the stall and laid down fresh hay. He knew he could leave the stallion out as long as he left the door open so Dracula could come back to his stall if he felt like it. All he needed to do was close the main door of the stable. "Okay, boy. I'll be out for a bit. I need to go find her. You understand. I'll be back later, okay?"

Dracula seemed to nod as he vocalized his permission for Mark to leave.

He headed for the garage and jumped into his old German BMW. It was a vanity purchase, but he liked the older models. He put a lot of money into keeping it up. The silver exterior shone, and the dark gray leather interior was kept clean and supple, in pristine condition. He started the engine, and with a happy shout, backed out before speeding off down the road. He headed straight for the Veleru compound hoping she was still there.

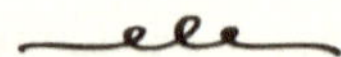

"Grandmama, I know I am right!" Dana sat across from Adina who shook her head.

"But we all saw him, Dana. He was most definitely still vampire. I, too, thought it might work, but only if we could have prevented the pact from being completed."

Meghan jumped in. "But that isn't how Magdalena explained it."

Dana took it up from there. "It is just like when he was made vampire. It was a process. It took a full day before he transformed into Strigoi. It makes sense it would take time to transform back to human."

Adina huffed. "We have no way of knowing if what you think is true. Do you even know where he lives?" She addressed Meghan who shook her head.

"No, but he said this all used to be his family's land. He still lives in the area, so it would seem he is somewhere close by. That's what he said. Do you have a phone book?"

Adina raised an eyebrow. "A phone listing... for a vampire?"

Meghan sighed. "I know. It was a longshot."

Cosmin walked in wiping dust from his face. He'd been out in the small winery where they processed the grapes grown on the land.

"Someone is coming,' he said.

"What? Who?" Stefan and Ilana asked simultaneously.

Cosmin folded his handkerchief. "I do not know. Too far down the road yet, but it is a car."

Sorin headed for the front door and stood staring out. "It's a silver car." He looked back inside. "Anyone know someone who drives a BMW?"

"No." Adina stood. Dana and Meghan followed as she made her way to Sorin. They spilled out onto the front porch watching the vehicle speed up the driveway.

The car pulled into the circular drive and slid to a stop kicking up dust. The dark tinted windows hid the identity of the driver.

Everyone waited to see who it was. The door opened and the driver stepped out.

There he stood, tall, strong, and devastatingly handsome in the sunshine. He wore blue jeans, black boots, and a cream-colored, cable-knit sweater. The wind gently lifted his dark chestnut hair sifting through it like a lover's fingers. A tentative smile spread across his lips as his eyes sought out the woman he loved.

"Mark!" she squeaked. Meghan pushed past Dana and Sorin running headlong into his outstretched arms.

They closed around her immediately, holding her tight. "Meghan! My Meghan!" He lifted her up and spun her around.

Her hands ran over his face, shoulders, arms. "You're real. You're human! I can feel your heartbeat," she said as she laid her hand on his hard chest.

"It beats for you, my love," he whispered.

"How? When?" She was full of questions, but his lips silenced her, claiming her mouth in a tender and loving kiss. With slow deliberation, Mark explored her lips.

In between thrilling nips, and sexy caresses he whispered, "So warm, so soft. So forgiving."

"I can't believe it." Meghan's voice broke on a sob.

"Don't cry, my love. Don't cry." He kissed her tears away. "Fate has given us a second chance. It has given me back my humanity. I can breathe, feel, and grow old." He pulled back and touched her face, staring into the depths of her beautiful brown eyes. "That is, if you... Will you grow old with me, Meghan?" he asked, suddenly nervous and unsure of himself.

Cosmin, Sorin, Dana, Stefan, Ilana, Alexandru, Marius, and Adina watched as the human who was a vampire, now human once more, waited for their Meghan to give her answer, for he was surely proposing.

"I think Anghelescu has waited long enough, Meghan." Adina chuckled.

Mark glanced at the old woman and smiled. He immediately returned his attention to his love. "So?"

Meghan leaned closer, her lips within a breath of his own, and smiled. "Yes."

A loud whoop went up behind them as Mark laid a kiss on her that weakened her knees. Filled with passion and joy, he held her close, whispering over and over again how much he loved her.

Adina reached for Cosmin's hand. "Gather the family. We have another ceremony to prepare for."

Dana giggled, and unable to contain herself any longer, ran for her friend, pushing Mark away. "Let someone else hug her, vampire."

Mark laughed. It was the first time the little gypsy had said that word with affection. Sorin and Stefan each pulled him in for bro hugs and handshakes. Ilana grabbed his hand, and peeked up at him, arms out.

"Welcome to our family Marku Anghelescu."

Mark let her hug him, feeling the love of family after so long. His heart felt like it might explode with joy. Tears filled his eyes.

"Why the tears?' Meghan wrapped her arms around him, concerned.

"I have been alone for so long, and now there is all of this." He looked around at the sea of faces surrounding them.

"Oh, my love." Meghan cupped his face. "You're not alone anymore. We are not alone."

"I know, but I wonder if I even deserve all this? The things I've done, Meghan..."

"Hey, look at me." She pulled his face to hers. "Magdalena told me something."

"What?"

"Your vampirism was caused by her curse, not Petrescu's. Nothing that you did during that time was on you. You were a weapon under her control, a means to protect her pact and end Petrescu. None of it was part of who you are, and not in any way a stain on your soul."

Skepticism warred in his eyes with hope. "Truly?"

"Yes. You were a good man before, and despite what she put you through, you held on to being a good man. You loved me, didn't you?"

He smiled. "Oh, yes. Always."

"She said the soulless cannot love. You always had your soul, and that soul loved me. That's a good thing."

His doubts melted away. "Now I know why I have always loved you." Mark tucked a strand of her honey-blonde hair behind her ear. "You are everything that is good. You are my blessing, and I will spend every day of the rest of my thankfully much shorter life proving it to you." He pulled her close and held her head to his heart. The simplicity of enjoying the moment without a hint of bloodlust was amazing. But there was still lust of another kind.

Dana tilted her head in the direction of the house indicating everyone should leave the two love birds alone. Cosmin chuckled and went inside. Stefan held Ilana's hand and they moved off to the guest house with Alexandru on their heels. Sorin stifled a snort and offered his arm to his grandmother.

Finally alone, Mark lifted Meghan's chin, staring down at her all the love he held within his heart for her throughout the ages. He kissed her slowly, softly, and tenderly. When he pulled back, her face was bemused. "Meghan?"

"Um hmm?" She smiled dreamily at her man.

"I'm cold... and hungry, I think. In fact, I think I am starving."

The look of both confusion and wonder on his face made her laugh. "Well, let's go inside and get you fed, and then later, I'll work on warming you up," she said with a saucy wink.

"I'd like that." He laughed, kissing her thoroughly again. "I love you, Meghan Hartley. Forever."

And without a doubt, she knew he meant it.

Also By Michele E. Gwynn

Get a FREE book by visiting my website at micheleegwynnau thor.com.

Checkpoint Novels

Exposed: The Education of Sarah Brown (novel)
The Evolution of Elsa Kreiss (novel)
The Redemption of Joseph Heinz (novel)
The Making of Herman Faust (prequel novella)

Green Beret Series

Rescuing Emma (18+)
Loving Leisl

Freeing Fatima

Saving Christmas

Loving Freddie

Saving Major Morgan (A Green Beret Series prequel novella)

Saving Isla (Coming Soon)

The Soldiers of PATCH-COM

Secondhand Soldier (18+)

Second Chance Soldier

Second Breath Soldier

Silent Night Soldier

C'est la Vie Soldier

The Harvest Trilogy

Harvest

Hybrids

Census

Section 5 (A Harvest Trilogy Spinoff)

Angelic Hosts Series

(Available Exclusively on my Substack for FREE)

Camael's Gift

Camael's Battle

Sophie's Wish
Nephilim Rising

Stand Alones

Darkest Communion (Paranormal Romance, 18+)
Waiting a Lifetime (Contemporary Romance, Mystical)
Hiring John (Romantic Comedy 18+)